ORPHAN GIRL'S DREAM

HISTORICAL VICTORIAN SAGA

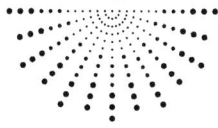

ROSIE SWAN

PUREREAD.COM

CONTENTS

Chapter 1	1
Chapter 2	9
Chapter 3	19
Chapter 4	29
Chapter 5	36
Chapter 6	44
Chapter 7	49
Chapter 8	57
Chapter 9	64
Chapter 10	71
Chapter 11	78
Chapter 12	86
Chapter 13	93
Chapter 14	100
Chapter 15	107
Chapter 16	113
Chapter 17	120
Chapter 18	127
Chapter 19	140
Chapter 20	147
Chapter 21	154
Chapter 22	162
Chapter 23	171
Chapter 24	177
Chapter 25	183
Chapter 26	189
Chapter 27	198
Chapter 28	204
Chapter 29	208
Love Victorian Romance?	213
Our Gift To You	215

CHAPTER ONE

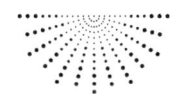

When Molly Thompson agreed to marry Richard Wilkins, she had few romantic notions about the match. Richard was a steady man with steady work at the docks, and Molly believed he could provide a steady life for the two of them that was so precious and rare in the poorer parts of Liverpool in those days. Richard was kind to her, and seemed to like her, and Molly liked him too. He made her laugh sometimes, and brought her flowers, and after the loss of her parents, Molly had little money with which to support herself and no future as an unmarried woman outside of the workhouse. Their courtship was brief, their wedding simple, and when they settled into Richard's small home together on the night after their marriage, Molly felt relieved that she had found a safe home and life for herself

But although Molly had few romantic notions about their marriage, she did not have *none*. She imagined that her husband would be kind to her, as he was before they married, that he might occasionally bring gifts home for her or compliment her on her dress or her cooking. She imagined a partnership with an element of sweetness to it, and a sense of safety that would colour all of their interactions together.

It took approximately a week after the wedding for Molly to learn that her new husband was a drunk. At first, Molly tried to accept this. All men had their flaws and their vices, and she had never expected her new husband to be perfect. Yes, he would stumble home in the middle of the night, mumbling to himself, and yes, he used much of their money on drink, but many women lived in worse situations. At least Molly had a roof over her head and enough food to fight the hunger away. Besides, Molly had worked in a rope factory on the dockyard for several years by that point, and she had not imagined leaving the work until she had children, so they could afford the extra expense.

A few weeks after that, she learned that he was a violent drunk, and that any small, imagined insult or failing on Molly's part was enough to trigger his anger. The first time, Molly merely dared to ask him if he had had a pleasant evening. He came stumbling in through the door at one in the morning, stinking of alcohol, but Molly would insist until she died that she had not meant the question in anything but earnest. It was lonely waiting at home, not knowing when her husband would appear, and she wished to connect with him somehow, to hear about his day. She had meant it as an honest inquiry, not as a rebuke or an insult.

Richard did not see it that way, and Molly's new black eye was a painful reminder of his disapproval. No one at work asked her about the obvious injury, but she thought she saw pity in some of their looks, and their whispered conversation often stopped when she came their way.

Still, Molly hoped that it had simply been an unfortunate incident and was not an omen of the future. And it was true that Richard was not always violent, even if he was almost always drunk. He never sought out Molly to hurt her. As long as she remained quiet, out of sight and out of mind, she continued relatively unmolested.

No, the worst element of her marriage, in Molly's mind, was the loneliness. She had married for financial reasons, yes, for the fear of ending up out on the streets, but she had also married for companionship. After her parents died, she felt utterly alone in the world, and although she occasionally joined in the gossip with the other women at the factory when the foreman was not looking, that was not a substitute for real connections. Although she had not grown up rich by any means, her family had been rich in love, and her heart ached at the loss of the peace it had brought her. She had spent her childhood knowing that there were people in this world who loved her and cared for her, knowing that she would be protected if she possibly could be; knowing, most of all, that she was not alone. Once her parents had died, she had ached for that feeling, but Richard was either unwilling or unable to provide it anew.

Most of the time, Richard did not speak to Molly at all, except perhaps to demand food or complain about how the world seemed out to get him. He barely seemed to consider Molly a person at all.

And Molly could not escape him. She had no living relatives or friends that she could turn to, and she lacked the money to help herself. Although she worked hard every day at the rope factory, her husband took all of her wages for himself. He spent most of the money on his drinks and his tobacco, barely leaving enough for Molly to stock the larder. If he had not been so fond of his food, Molly thought he would probably not have left enough even for that. Certainly, on the days he chose to eat outside of the house, he did not leave any money behind so that Molly could eat.

The result of all this tragedy was that, at twenty-two, Molly Wilkins already felt as tired and as bitter as she imagined was more fitting a woman three times her age. She was overworked and underfed, her fingers raw from weaving the rope fibres at the factory and her skin bruised from her husband's cruel grip. She did not even dream of a better future any longer. She trudged through the days, knowing that each one would be the same as the one before it and the one that would follow after.

Molly always hurried home after her shift at the factory was done. Even if Richard rarely returned home on an evening instead of travelling to the pub, he always expected *her* to be there, and he would be furious if he stepped through the front door and found her absent.

It was the same on the spring evening upon which this story begins. Molly walked quickly along the docks in the grey evening light, her woollen shawl pulled tight around her shoulders to fight off the chill that still hung in the air, even in April. The lantern lighters had done their work, and the gleam of the streetlights cut through the gently rolling fog, leading Molly home. A few sailors shouted at Molly as she hurried past, as they often did, and Molly shot them a scowl that could freeze the blood. The men only laughed at her expression and turned their attention to another target, and Molly rubbed her hands together against the cold, thinking of the few items in her otherwise sparse larder and desperately hoping she might make a meal of them.

If she was lucky, she would be asleep before her husband returned. She usually was, these past few weeks. But eventually her luck would have to run out.

"Excuse me, miss." A tall man approached her, and she slowed when she saw the gentle, unassuming expression on his face. He had both the look and the smell of a sailor, as though the salt from the sea air had seeped permanently into his sun-weathered skin. He was older than Molly by at least a decade, and his dress and manner were both those of a man with a decent, if not a rich, upbringing. He was the sort of man who might become a captain, Molly thought at once, if he did not settle down for a life away from the sea.

"Can I help you?" Molly asked him. The man smiled.

"I hope so, miss," he said. "I'm looking for the dockmaster's office. You couldn't point me in the right direction, could you?"

"It's just there," Molly said, pointing the way, "but I think the dockmaster will have gone home for the day by now. He never stays very late if he can help it."

The man swore softly, but when Molly flinched slightly, he smiled again, a little ruefully. "My apologies, miss," he said. "I really did wish to talk with him. I suppose I'll be back tomorrow."

Molly could not think what to say in response to that, so she simply nodded at him and continued on her way again.

Her hands felt fair numb by the time she reached her front door, and she struggled with the lock for a moment before realising it was already open. Her heart sank as she pushed the door open, revealing her husband slumped over at the kitchen table.

"You're home late," he muttered at her. "Where you been?"

"Work," she said simply. "Sometimes they keep us late."

"You not been talking to anybody?" For a wild moment, Molly imagined that he must know about the stranger she'd spoken to on the docks. But that was ridiculous. Even if he did know about it, which was impossible, it had hardly even been a conversation. She certainly had not done anything wrong.

"No," Molly said. "I'll make dinner."

Richard held out one sweaty, dirty hand, palm up.

"Payday isn't until tomorrow," Molly said quietly.

"You must have something leftover."

"I spent it all on food," Molly said. In truth, she had a few coins left in her pocket, enough to buy him a drink or two at least, but she was loath to part with them. He would take away all of her earnings tomorrow anyway.

Richard slammed his fist down onto the table, and Molly jumped. She braced herself for the fury that was bound to follow, but then Richard just snorted as he stood and began to make his way to the door. "I'll borrow from Mickey," Richard said. "He owes me one." He spoke so quietly that Molly wasn't certain whether he was addressing her or himself. Either way, he did not bid her goodbye as he left.

Once he was gone, Molly sank into her chair and pressed her head into her hands. At least she had a home, she told herself. There was no point in dreaming of anything different.

CHAPTER TWO

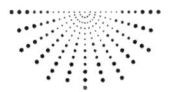

Molly saw the stranger the following evening, too. The fog was a little less thick, but the wind was harsher, and she was hunched over slightly against the cold, so she did not notice him until she had almost bumped into him. When she did spot him, she was so startled that she jumped and gasped.

"I'm sorry, miss," the man said. His hands reached out to steady her shoulders, and Molly's heartrate picked up even more when she felt his warmth seeping through his gloves and her shawl. He released her quickly and took a respectful step back. "I didn't mean to startle you."

Molly just shook her head, struggling for words. "No, I'm sorry," she said. "I should have been watching where I was going."

"I just wanted to thank you," the man said, "for your help yesterday. I spoke to the dockmaster this morning."

"Oh," Molly said. That did not seem worth seeking her out again to thank her, but perhaps, she reasoned, he had simply noticed her by coincidence again and decided it would be polite to greet her. "I'm glad to hear it."

"The name's Billy," the man said. He held out a hand for Molly to shake. Molly took it, a little reluctantly. He had a firm grip and a broad smile, and as their eyes met, Molly felt a slight flutter in her chest. He had an enchanting smile, warm and genuine, the kindness radiating from his eyes.

"Molly," Molly said. "Molly Wilkins."

"It's a pleasure to meet you, Molly Wilkins," he said. Then he looked about and let out a breath. "Chilly, isn't it?" he said. "I could really do with a coffee. Is there a stall, do you know, anywhere around here?"

Molly nodded. "Mrs Hooley keeps a stall on the edge of the docks," she said.

"Do you recommend it?" he asked, with a slightly mischievous twist to his smile.

"I do," Molly said. In all honesty, she rarely ever stopped there. She did not have the pennies to spare for a warming coffee, no matter how common it might be among her fellow workers, and no matter how cold the Liverpool air could turn. She had indulged in the drinks occasionally, before the loss of her parents, before her marriage, but it had been several years now.

Billy grinned at her. "I'd appreciate it if you could show me," he said. "This place is a maze. Let me repay your kindness with a hot drink. It's far too cold for a lovely young woman like you to go without."

Molly felt herself blushing. That was the moment, she knew, where she should mention that she was married and excuse herself from the conversation. But she remained silent. Billy had not said anything inappropriate, or even suggestive. It seemed unlikely that he could think she was lovely to look at, but flattery was common enough, even among acquaintances, and she suddenly, desperately wanted to say yes to his proposal. She spent no time to herself and had no conversation that was worthwhile these days.

If Richard were already home, then he could wait.

"Yes," she said. "That would be nice."

Billy offered her the crook of his arm, and she took it with a smile.

"Are you new to Liverpool then?" Molly asked him as they walked.

"I've visited occasionally," Billy said. "Life as a sailor takes you to all the ports, and I've done the route between here and New York more times than I can count. First time staying on land, though."

"New York!" Molly said. She struggled to imagine what a faraway place must be like. "It must have been exciting."

"It was at first," Billy said. "But it wears on you, being at sea all the time. Makes you yearn for a home. A warm hearth and the right woman to share it with."

Molly found herself blushing again. But of course, she reminded herself, he could never mean her. Even if she was not married, which she *was*, she had never been the sort of girl to attract a well-spoken, successful sailor, not even before her marriage drained half of the life from her and she was in the prime of her beauty.

"Well, I hope you find that soon," Molly said.

"I do as well," he said. "It's why I'm here. I'm tired of life on the sea. I'm looking to settle down."

"And you chose Liverpool, out of all the places in the world?"

"Why not?" Billy said. "It certainly has its upsides." He gave Molly another bright smile, and Molly hesitantly returned it.

He ordered them both hot cups of coffee, as he had promised, and they lingered by Mrs Hooley's stall to drink them. Mrs Hooley slightly raised an eyebrow at the sight of Molly's companion, but she did not comment, which Molly appreciated.

"Have you ever travelled?" Billy asked her. Molly shook her head.

"I've never been outside of Liverpool," she admitted. "I used to dream of going to London, when I was younger, but… I don't think it's possible now."

"Someone should take you to London," Billy said decisively.

Molly could only smile in return.

After they finished their coffees, Molly thanked Billy and bid him farewell, thinking that she was unlikely to ever see him again. She hurried home in the fierce wind, and her heart sank when she saw Richard at the table again, waiting for her.

"You're late again," he grunted. "You get paid?"

Molly did not want to respond to that, so she removed her shawl and hurried over to the stove.

"You gone deaf, girl?" Richard said. He swayed slightly as he stood. "Where's the money?"

"I won't talk to you when you're like this," Molly said, with as much calm dignity as she could muster.

Richard crossed the room in an instant. He seized Molly's wrist hard enough to bruise, and she struggled not to gasp as he pulled her toward him. She could feel his warm breath on her face and smell the liquor he had already consumed. Had he even been to work today, or had he simply stayed home to drink?

"Don't talk back to me," he spat. "Everything that belongs to you belongs to me, remember? *You* belong to me." He shoved his free hand into her pocket and pulled out the coins she had been given by the factory foreman barely an hour before. "This everything?" he asked.

Molly nodded.

"It's not much," Richard said. His grip on her wrist tightened. "You lying to me? You been slacking off?"

"No," Molly gasped.

"Maybe you haven't even been going to work," he said, pulling her even closer.

"I have," Molly said. "I have, this is everything."

Richard stared at her for a long moment, and Molly flinched, certain he was going to hit her. Then he released her wrist and turned away, muttering to himself. Molly said nothing as he threw open the door and slammed it shut behind him, probably off to spend all her money on drink and gaming, and then return to punish her for not having the coin to put food on the table.

Molly put her head in her hands. Tears burned in her eyes. Her wrist ached, and when she looked at it, she could see purple bruises already blooming where her husband had grabbed her. Her shoulders shook, and suddenly her home felt far too constricting. She could not catch her breath in here. It was a prison, and the worst part was that she had walked into it willingly, expecting it to bring freedom instead.

She grabbed her shawl and wrapped it tightly around her shoulders before heading back out into the dusk. She did not know where she was going. She just knew that she could not possibly remain inside another moment.

She found herself walking vaguely back in the direction of Mrs Hooley's coffee stall, but Mrs Hooley had closed for the night. The streetlamps glowed around her, and the wind pulled at her hair, loosening it from the pins that had held it the entirety of this long, long day. She turned past the docks, where she was certain to get unwelcome shouts from lingering sailors, and made her way farther along, to where the pier stood.

"Molly?" She did not hear the shout at first, too wrapped up in her thoughts and her tears. But then the person shouted again, louder, and she stopped and turned.

Billy was hurrying across the street towards her.

"What are you doing out this late?" he said. "I thought you went home." He stopped suddenly once he saw her clearly. "What happened to you?" he asked. "You're crying."

Molly just shrugged. She couldn't think how to put her misery into words.

"Oh, hey, now," Billy said. He put a comforting hand on her shoulder. "It'll be all right, Miss Molly." Then he spotted the bruises on her arm, and his expression turned dark. "What happened? Who did that to you?"

"My husband," Molly said quietly, through her tears. She blushed, knowing that this strange man would think she had misled him, knowing he would storm away or worse now that the truth was out.

He did none of those things. His expression turned even darker, and he reached out gently to take her wrist and inspect the bruises.

"No husband should do something like that," he said. "No matter what the situation." He frowned. "Was it because you were late home? Did I cause this?"

"No," Molly said, shaking her head and sniffing. "No, there's no—nothing ever really causes it. I didn't bring home enough money from the factory for him this week." Her heart started to beat faster again as she thought back to the encounter. "He left me with no money to buy food," she said. "Hopefully he'll eat at the pub, but—"

"Then let's get you something to eat," Billy said. "I'm staying in the inn just over that way, and they do an excellent shepherd's pie."

Molly shook her head again. "I couldn't," she said. "I don't have any money—"

"I'll take care of that."

"It wouldn't be proper," she whispered.

"It's a public meeting place," Billy said, "and you need to eat. I won't leave you while you're this upset. What's not proper is a husband treating you this way. *That's* what the gossip should be about."

"Oh, don't tell anybody," Molly said, clutching her shawl tighter around herself. "Please." It wouldn't make any difference—the marriage was legal and binding—and she would just receive even more pity and disdain from people who knew.

Billy considered her for a moment, and then nodded. "All right," he said. "I won't say a word. Come on now."

Molly followed him to the public house where he was staying and collapsed gratefully into a wooden chair at a table by the fire. Billy went to ask the landlord for some food, and Molly gripped her shawl and looked around, as though her husband might be lurking in a corner. He would never patronise such a fine establishment, where the drinking was subdued and gaming was clearly forbidden, but she did not quite trust her own luck in avoiding him and his acquaintances. But the inn was quiet, with only a few weary-looking travellers sitting alone at separate tables, and slowly, Molly began to relax.

It wasn't until she took her first bite of shepherd's pie that she realised how hungry she was. She felt drained, but the pie was rich, the potatoes surprisingly fluffy, and every bite seemed to give her new strength. Billy sat in thoughtful silence while she ate, but as she calmed down, she began to realise once again how inappropriate it was for her to be here.

"Did that help?" Billy asked her, after the final bite.

"Yes," Molly said. "Yes, thank you. Please, when I have the coin, please let me repay you—"

"Not a chance," Billy said. "We're friends now, aren't we? Friends help one another. And even if that wasn't true, what sort of person would I be if I left a poor young woman crying in the street?"

"I'm just so embarrassed," Molly said softly.

"You have nothing to be embarrassed about," Billy said. "It's your husband who should be ashamed."

Molly stood up, feeling herself blushing again. "I should really be getting home," she said. "He won't be back until late now, but—I should rest." She felt strangely flustered. "Thank you again for your kindness."

"Any time, Molly," Billy said, standing too. "Do you need any company on your walk home? I would hate for you to get hurt1."

"No," Molly said quickly. "I'll be all right." She could not have any neighbours see them together, even if nothing inappropriate had happened. "But thank you."

CHAPTER THREE

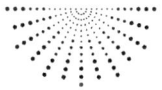

Molly saw Billy every day after that. He never delayed her long, but he was a constant presence, asking her about her well-being and her plans for each day. On Friday, he brought her a bag of boiled sweets from the corner shop, as though they were childhood friends hungry for a treat after running in the mud, and Molly savoured every drop of sugar as they emptied the paper bag together.

On Monday, he brought her a single rose, a beautiful, delicate thing, its thorns trimmed away. Billy insisted that he had not intended to buy it, but that the street seller had seemed to need the money more than he did. "Besides," he said. "It's beautiful. Just like you."

Molly blushed and looked away, but she did not have the heart to tell him to stop, even if it was improper. She gave the flower to a forlorn-looking girl before returning home, knowing that she dared not let her husband see it, but the memory of it kept her warm and strong through the entire rest of the night. It had had such pure beauty.

It was, she thought, not really like her at all.

But still, Billy returned. He brought hot cups of coffee and cakes and bread to eat. One day, he even brought her a blue ribbon as a gift.

"I couldn't resist buying it," he told her, as he pressed it into her hand. "It's the exact same colour as your eyes."

He tied it to the end of her braid, like they were a young couple courting, and Molly blushed with pleasure.

It was harmless, she told herself, every time she saw him. She was so lonely that it was a physical ache in her chest, and it was warming to meet someone who actually seemed to appreciate her company. Yes, he was a man, and he was acting as though he were wooing her, but he knew she was married. He understood the limits of this flirtation.

Her husband never showed her a single drop of care or attention, and he certainly found his pleasure elsewhere. He found companionship in drink and gaming, and probably in other women too, although Molly had no proof of that, beyond his lack of interest in her. Was it not a crime on his part for him to neglect her like this? He was failing in his duty as a man and as a husband. Was Molly supposed to live the rest of her life without a single flicker of warmth or affection from anyone, because of her husband's failings?

It was harmless, she told herself. She was not doing anything truly improper. The only person who would be hurt was Molly herself, once Billy inevitably left and she was alone again.

Two weeks after she first met Billy, Molly left the factory late, her whole body aching from a day's hard work. The sun had already set, and the streetlamps flickered in the mist, adding an eerie feel to the chilly autumn night. It was her husband's payday, so she knew he would not even bother to return home before heading out to drink. She would have the entire evening to herself. The thought was not as comforting as it should have been. She would be free of his oppressive presence for a while, but there would be nothing to fill that hole of loneliness in her chest. Not for the first time, Molly wondered how long she could possibly continue like this.

She found Billy by Mrs Hooley's coffee stall, and his warm smile was enough to melt some of her loneliness away. "Molly!" he said. "The sight of you is enough to chase off the cold. Or maybe that's the coffee."

She smiled back at him and did not argue when he turned back to Mrs Hooley and ordered a drink for her as well. Molly held it with both hands, letting the warmth seep through the cup and her gloves.

"I was hoping I would see you," Billy said. "Do you have a little time tonight? There's something I wanted to show you."

Molly nodded, emboldened by the heat of the drink in her hands. "Yes," she said. "Yes, I'm free tonight."

Mrs Hooley did not comment on the two of them walking off together again, but Molly noticed the way she frowned.

There is nothing to disapprove of, Molly wanted to turn back and say. Somehow, she did not think stating that would convince anyone.

They walked the quiet streets, following the glow of the lamplight. Molly found herself content to walk in silence, simply savouring his company, trusting him not to lead her astray.

After about ten minutes of walking, the streets began to grow more crowded with pedestrians again. She could hear music drifting on the air, not too far away. She looked at Billy, the question in her eyes, and he grinned.

"You didn't know about the Autumn's Fayre?" he asked. She shook her head. "I thought you probably hadn't. Which is why I thought perhaps we should attend."

Molly hesitated. A voice in her head, small but insistent, told her that she should not be here. She should not be attending a festival with a man who brought her gifts and was not her husband. Someone might see them. And even if no one noticed them, it was still improper, was it not? Wasn't it breaking her vows and her faith to her husband, in spirit if not in deed?

Yet when Billy held out his arm to her in invitation, like a fine gentleman about to escort his lady to the ball, Molly could not resist accepting it. A warm thrill ran through her as she tucked her arm into the crook of his elbow, and they set off after the music together.

The band played a jaunty jig, all fiddle and harpsichord, and Molly found herself springing slightly to the beat. People danced in the area before the stage, and stalls lined the street, selling more hot drinks and food and various handmade goods than Molly could never dream of affording. Billy bought them a paper bag full of hot doughnuts to share. They were so hot that they almost burned the roof of Molly's mouth, but she ate them hungrily with one hand, still clinging to Billy with the other.

Billy purchased some hot cider too, and although Molly generally did not approve of alcohol, considering her husband's relationship to it, the stall was so festive, and the drink was so warming that she found herself happy to drink it. It warmed her inside almost more than Billy's smile did, and her worries began to melt away as she sipped it.

Once they had finished their refreshments, Billy's arm shifted, and he took Molly's hand. She yelped in surprise as he hauled her forward, racing toward the dancing. "Billy!" she cried, but she could not help laughing. "Billy, wait!"

"Don't you want to dance?"

She did want to dance. And with the heat of the cider inside her and the sight of Billy's excited smile filling her chest with delight, she could not think of a single reason not to do so.

They danced a jig together, Molly's skirts flying around them, and all Molly's exhaustion from her day's work vanished beneath the rhythm of the music and the joy in her heart. They spun around together, not really knowing the steps but inventing them when necessary, until Molly was breathless with laughter. The stars gleamed overhead, and Molly's heart felt light and free.

When the music stopped, Billy was holding her close, their chests almost touching. Could he feel how hard her heart was racing? He smiled at her, his expression soft and fond, and he glanced down at her lips.

All at once, he was kissing her. His lips were warm and firm, his hands gentle around her waist, and *oh*, Molly thought. She had not known that it could feel like this. Kisses with Richard had always been perfunctory, with no real feeling behind them, if he kissed her at all. She had just assumed that that was the way kisses were.

This was different. The rest of the world seemed to fade away as heat spread through her. She felt safe and warm and *wanted*, and the sensation was so good and so unfamiliar that tears sprang to her eyes.

It only lasted a few moments, before Molly's thoughts caught up with her, and she realised what precisely they were doing. She leapt back with a gasp, her hand flying to her mouth. Billy just looked at her, seeming slightly dazed. He was smiling, but his smile faded as he registered the expression on her face.

"Molly…" he said.

She turned and ran. She darted between the other revellers until she was free of the crowd, and then she darted down a side street, her legs moving as fast as she could work them.

She could hear Billy running after her. "Molly, wait!"

She kept running, but Billy was much faster than she was, and he soon caught up with her. He caught her elbow in his hand, and she spun around, her sight blurry with tears.

"I can't," she gasped at him. "I can't."

"I'm sorry, Molly," he said. "That was too forward of me. I didn't mean to upset you."

"Why would you kiss me?" she asked him, the words fierce. Despair was bubbling up inside her, threatening to overwhelm her. He had ruined it. She had been able to lie to herself until that moment, to convince herself that it was all innocent, that she was doing nothing wrong at all. But now that he had kissed her, the truth was laid bare, and it *hurt*. It hurt how much she cared for him, and how desperately she wanted to be with him. He was a chance at happiness, but she could not accept him. She had already married Richard.

"I kissed you because I wanted to," Billy said softly. "You were smiling, and you looked beautiful, and I really wanted to kiss you. I've wanted to for a while."

"But I'm *married*," Molly said.

"And what a husband he is," Billy jeered. "You can hardly call it a marriage. You deserve better than him, Molly. You should be with *me*."

She gaped at him. It was the first time he had declared his intentions so clearly, and for a moment, the force of his words stole her breath away.

"You—you want to be with me?" she whispered.

"Of course, I do," Billy said. He cupped her cheek in the palm of his hand. "I love you, Molly. You're the most wonderful woman I've ever met. I want to settle down with you and have a family. Here, or in London, or wherever you like. New York, if you prefer it."

His words were so appealing, so soothing, but she forced herself to shake her head. "I can't," she said. "We can't. You know we can't. Even if Richard is—even if he is not the husband I had hoped he would be, I am still married."

"I don't care about that," Billy said. He took her hand in his, squeezing it gently. "Listen to me. I don't care. We can go far away, Molly, where no one knows who we are. We can tell everyone that we are married, and your husband will never find us. He'll never be able to hurt you again, and we'll be happy."

Molly closed her eyes. She could picture it perfectly. The two of them walking arm in arm together down unfamiliar streets, laughing and smiling together. Evenings spent curled up by the fire while their children played. A life where she never felt lonely again. Molly had never been particularly romantic, had never believed that such things were even really possible, but in that moment, she felt certain that nothing would be so wonderful as to get swept away. Her heart yearned for it.

But her head knew that such a thing was impossible. She pulled her hand away from Billy's, shaking her head. "It would be a sin," she said.

"God would forgive you," Billy said. "He would understand. He would not want you to suffer like you are. He would want you to help yourself."

But Molly continued to shake her head. "I cannot," she said. "Please do not ask it of me."

"I am asking it of you," Billy said. "I will not stop asking it of you. Please listen to me, Molly. We belong together."

She stepped back, still shaking her head. "I am sorry, Billy," she said. "Please—please do not make this harder than it already is. Please."

Before he could reply, she turned and ran again. This time, he did not follow her.

CHAPTER FOUR

Richard was not at the house when Molly returned. She toed off her shoes and then collapsed into bed without changing, weighed down by her despair.

Her husband, when he did next see her, did not seem to notice the difference. Just as he had not noticed or cared about her increased happiness over the past few weeks, he did not consider it worth his notice that she was despairing again. Molly's coworkers at the factory noticed that she was a little quieter than usual, but Molly was always quiet, and they all knew what a brute her husband could be, so they said nothing about it to her.

Molly still saw Billy, but they did not speak. He haunted her, like the spirit of what her life could and should have been. She saw him when she walked home from the factory every evening, and he nodded and touched his hat to her. Molly found it difficult to pass him without approaching him, but she forced herself to do so, day after day. If they spoke, she knew her resolve would shatter.

Soon, she knew, he would move on. For all of his pretty words, he would meet another woman, one more worthy of him, and he would no longer linger at the docks for a glimpse at her face. He might even leave Liverpool altogether.

That is good, she told herself, over and over. It was what needed to happen. It was for the best.

Still, it hurt more than she could have imagined when, a week after their kiss, Molly did not catch so much as a glimpse of Billy on her walk home. She could not help looking for him out of the corner of her eye as she walked, but he was not on the docks, or at Mrs Hooley's, where he often lingered for a coffee around the time that she left the factory.

He was gone. He had grown tired of the waiting, and now she might not ever see his smile again.

Her whole body felt heavy as she stepped through the front door of her home. She was so distracted that she almost did not notice the bottle flying towards her. She ducked just in time, and it struck the wall beside the doorframe. It did not shatter, but the wall was slightly dented where it hit.

Richard was standing by the fireplace, swaying. She could smell the alcohol on him from the doorway. "You're late," he shouted at her. His words slurred together. "Where have you been?"

"I've been at the factory," Molly said sharply. She was in no mood to appease this disgusting boor of a man, not when she had lost so much to his selfishness and rage. "Earning the money to pay for your drink."

She almost expected him to charge at her for her defiance, but he just laughed. "So you do," he said, almost to himself. "My little wife. Working hard every day to keep me in comfort."

Molly scowled at him as she strode across the room toward the larder. "Did you leave any money to stock the kitchen?" she asked him. "Or did you spend it all on whatever you've been drinking today?"

He snorted. "It's all mine," he said. "You're mine. The money is mine. I can use it however I please. You want to eat, you'll have to go out and earn more." He leered at her, and then laughed again. "You'd have trouble though, wouldn't you? I don't need to worry. No one would pay any money for *you*. How did I end up with such a plain wife?"

"You married me," Molly said. She kept her back to him, squeezing her hands into fists to stop them from shaking. How dare he express disappointment in her, after how he had failed and mistreated her? She had tried her hardest for him. She had given up Billy for him. It would never be enough.

"I did," Richard said. "And what a mistake that was."

"Well, believe me," Molly said. "I'm not happy about it either."

He crossed the room in seconds, despite his unsteadiness on his feet. His meaty hand closed around Molly's upper arm hard enough to bruise as he wrenched her around to face him. "Think you could've done better than me, do you?" he said. His eyes were slightly unfocussed, and the smell of alcohol on his breath was almost suffocating. "No one else would take you, Molly. Not even the whorehouses would want you."

She wrenched her arm out of his grip, fighting back the tears that burned in her eyes. "I thought you were at work today," she said. "How did you find time to drink so much?"

"Job's over," Richard said. "Next one won't start for a time, and the boys and I wanted to celebrate."

"When do you ever not?" Molly murmured, desperately fighting to remain calm. *This is my life*, she thought. *This is the path that I have chosen.*

She hated it. Death might be preferable to this lonely, painful misery.

Richard grabbed her chin in his meaty hand. The gesture was a cruel imitation of the way that Billy had touched her, that night she'd cried after the fair. "You trying to look down on me?" he said, his voice low and threatening. "You think you're better than me?"

Molly tried to shake her head, but his grip on her chin was like a vice, holding her in place.

"Well?" he almost shouted.

"No," she whispered. "I don't."

"I should turn you out onto the street," he said. "It's only out of the goodness of my heart that I let you stay here at all. You know that, don't you? You belong to me, Molly. *Mrs Wilkins*." He almost spat the words, the title coming out in a mockery of affection. "Nobody else in this world cares about you. No one is there to protect you. You're *mine*. So, you think on that, before you go judging me. I'm the only thing that stands between you and starvation on the street."

She pulled her head free of his grip. "Sometimes I think I would rather starve on the streets," she spat at him. "Anything must be better than being married to *you*."

She expected the strike. She almost welcomed it. His hand caught her around the face, and blood burst from her lip as she staggered back.

"Now look!" Richard hissed. "Look what you forced me to do."

Molly stumbled backward toward the front door. Her whole body was shaking, telling her to run. Nothing could be worse than this. Richard was not worth keeping faith for. Not when she might be *happy* elsewhere.

She burst back out into the chilly night. Once on the street, she began to run, half stumbling in her haste. Billy had said he loved her. But for the first time since they met, she had not seen him. Had he left Liverpool, believing there was no hope? Was it already too late?

Molly realised she was crying. She rubbed her eyes with the back of her hand and paused beneath a streetlamp to catch her breath.

Was she really going to do this? Go to Billy, abandon her husband, live in sin for the chance at a better life?

Her head still rang from Richard's strike, and her stomach ached with the fear that Billy was already gone. Yes, she thought. This was what she wanted. It was the only choice she had.

She hurried to the inn that he had taken her to, a couple of weeks ago. He had said he was saying there, had he not? Molly could not quite remember, but it was as good a place to start searching as any. She steeled herself to ask the landlord after a tenant named Billy, knowing how it would make her appear, but to her surprise and relief, she spotted Billy as soon as she walked inside. He was sitting at a table alone, reading a newspaper and nursing a drink.

He was educated, then, Molly thought as she slowly crossed the room. Better educated than she was. It seemed impossible that he could desire to be with someone such as her, and yet….

She was still a few paces away when Billy looked up. For a moment, he looked too surprised for words, and then a kind smile spread across his face. "Molly!" he said. "I didn't think I would see you again." Then his smile faded as he got a closer look at her face. "Molly," he said again. "What happened to you?"

"My husband," she said. She crossed the remaining space between them. "You were right," she added, taking his hand in both of hers. "Everything you told me was right. I cannot continue living like this. I want to be with *you*."

Billy's entire face lit up at her declaration. Molly would be able see that face for the rest of her days. Her chest felt warm at the thought. Things would be better now.

"Are you certain?" he asked her. She nodded. She could feel herself smile as Billy surged up out of his seat and pulled her into a kiss, in plain view of the entire inn. Another customer whistled, and Billy backed off, his hands cupping her chin.

"Shall we go upstairs, my lady?" he asked her.

Molly nodded and took his hand.

CHAPTER FIVE

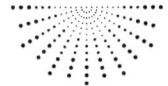

The next morning, Molly awoke alone. The mattress felt unfamiliar beneath her, and she sat up in a panic, looking around, wondering where she was.

Then she remembered. Billy. She had run away from Richard and her terrible old life. Everything would be different now.

She stretched out the knot in her shoulder as she looked around. She must have slept more deeply than she had in years, because the sun had already risen, casting bleary morning light across the room. Molly would be late for work, if she intended to return there. Perhaps she should, until she got her full week's pay again. Richard would not look for her for a while, she was certain. He might not even remember where she worked.

Billy was not in the room with her. He must have headed downstairs to eat breakfast, she thought, or maybe he had some employment he'd taken up since arriving in the city. She had never asked him.

But as Molly rose and slowly dressed in last night's clothes, she realised that Billy's possessions were all gone. The room was neat beyond her presence. There were no spare clothes, no personal trinkets, not even a sack where things might have been stored away.

Molly's stomach sank. But she was just being silly, she told herself. Billy loved her. He wanted to be with her. He must have needed to leave, temporarily, but he would be back.

The door to the room burst open, and Molly spun to face it, her heart leaping in anticipation. But it was not Billy. An unfamiliar woman strode into the room, a pile of sheets in her arms. She stopped when she saw Molly.

"What're you doing in here?"

"I—" Molly blushed. "I'm staying here."

The woman snorted. "You are not," she said. "The man renting this room paid up and left this morning."

"He—left?" Molly's hands shook. But that could not be true. It was a misunderstanding. Or—or he was out preparing for their new life together.

"Yes," the woman said. "And you better leave too, if you know what's good for you. I've already got this room rented out again, and I have work to do."

"But…" None of it made sense. "Did he say he would be back?"

"No." She gave Molly an assessing look. "Whoever he was, girl, I reckon he's gotten what he wanted. Take my advice and learn from this. Never trust a sailor."

"He wasn't a sailor," Molly said. "He'd—he'd left that work."

"I believe that's what he told you," the woman said. She placed the sheets down on a chair and then turned back to Molly. "But I don't much care for what happened here. I have work to do. I suggest you get going, girl."

Molly found herself nodding. She picked up her shawl and wrapped it around herself as she headed to the door on shaky legs.

"Don't worry yourself," the woman said, as Molly reached the door. "I have discretion. It's part of the work of a landlady. Even if I knew who you were—and I don't—your secrets would be safe with me."

Molly nodded. She could not speak. Her throat was too dry to form words. Then she turned and hurried from the room.

She went to the rope factory. What else could she do? She could not go home, and she did not know where to search for Billy, other than on the docks. The foreman shouted at her for her lateness, and Molly feared that she would lose her position, but she managed to make her excuses by blaming *women's troubles*, and the foreman was uncomfortable enough with this answer that he ended up just nodding brusquely and gesturing her on to work.

It was not even entirely a lie.

Molly fell into the rhythm of her work for the rest of the day, but her thoughts returned, again and again, to Billy. She felt a terrible fear in her stomach, a dread that she did not want to name. But she refused to believe that she had been tricked. Billy would not do that to her. He had told her that he loved her. He had promised he would be her happiness.

By the time the workday was over, Molly felt sick with her worry. She looked around the docks as she stepped out of the factory, desperately hoping for a glimpse of that familiar face, but he was not there.

She walked home slowly, desperately trying to think of where he might be. She did not dare return to the inn again. She passed by Mrs Hooley's, and even asked after him, but Mrs Hooley said she had not seen him since very early that morning. She gave Molly a pitying look too, and Molly tried to keep her expression as neutral as possible as she bid the woman goodnight. Pity would do nothing for her now.

She had been dreading returning home, but when she opened the front door of the house she had intended to never enter again, Richard was not there.

When he did finally return, he did not mention the fight of the previous night or Molly's absence. Molly thought he might have drunk so much that he could not even remember it.

It was a small mercy, but a mercy, nonetheless.

The following morning, Molly set out early. Gathering her courage, she went to the dockmaster's office to ask after Billy. He had been wanting to meet with the dockmaster when she first met him, after all, and the man must know most of the goings-on in his domain.

But the dockmaster could not recall any strangers coming to speak to him who were named Billy, or William either. When he asked Molly for the man's surname, Molly realised she had never learned it. She invented some excuse about looking for a man who had cheated her husband out of some money, and if the dockmaster did not believe her, he was at least too polite to say so to her face. He told her, not unkindly, that it was unlikely the man would show his face again, if he was even still in Liverpool at all. When in desperation, Molly asked if any large crews had left the previous day, the dockmaster confirmed that a steamer had departed for New York around noon after a couple of weeks in port.

It was not proof that Billy had left, and yet it was. Either she believed that some things he had told her were true, in which case it seemed most likely that he had left on that ship, or she accepted that it had all been lies, which guaranteed that he never intended to stay.

She had been his entertainment during his shore leave, she thought, hugging herself as she thanked the dockmaster for his time and hurried away. A challenge. See how far he could seduce the sad young woman whose husband did not love her before time ran out.

Part of her still wanted to believe that there was some hope there. Maybe an accident had befallen him, and he was recovering. Maybe he had been called out of Liverpool on business so suddenly that he could not inform her, but he would return. She clung to each thought like a lifeline, even as she knew, deep in her heart, that it was all untrue. Even someone with semi-good intentions would not have lied as he had. Even a common scoundrel, interested in a repeated fling in port, would have bid her goodbye before leaving, making promises he never intended to keep.

She had been deceived.

The days passed slowly after that. Molly followed the routine of her daily life, rising, working, cooking when she could, and sleeping just to rise again and do it all the following day, but everything felt empty now, shaded in grey. For a few short weeks, she had felt wanted. For a few hours, she had felt hope. Now it was all gone, lost so completely that Molly sometimes wondered if she had imagined it all. She could not stop herself from looking for Billy every time she walked home, and she lingered by Mrs Hooley's coffee stall, even though she had no coins to spend, but Billy was long gone, and her dreams had gone with him.

Molly was not surprised, therefore, when she began to feel physically unwell a few weeks later. She barely had the will to eat since Billy left her, and her stomach constantly churned. Nausea and dizziness seemed like the natural consequences of her heartbreak.

When her monthly courses did not appear, again, she did not think it unusual. They had always been irregular, thanks to the lack of steady food since her marriage, and the same despair that made her careless when counting the days seemed to explain its absence once she realised it was late.

But the weeks passed, and although Molly's nausea faded, her courses did not return. In quiet moments by herself, she found herself pressing her hand to her stomach. Had it grown? Could she feel any flutterings of movement inside?

Four months after Billy left her, Molly finally scraped together enough money to visit a midwife, and had her worst fears confirmed. She was pregnant.

CHAPTER SIX

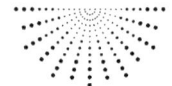

Her pregnancy should not have been as fearful a realisation as it was. She was married, after all. Everyone would naturally assume that the child belonged to Richard, and although the thought of that beast having any claim over her baby turned Molly's stomach, her reputation would remain unharmed.

But Richard would know the truth. He might hide it from his associates, to protect his own pride, but he would know that the child could not be his. Molly seemed to repulse him. They had not been intimate as husband and wife for the past six months at least, and although Richard's drink could make him forgetful, she did not think he was likely to forget this disdainful distance.

She might convince him otherwise, but it would require her to lie in words as well as in deeds. It would only compound her sin. It would be wisest for her to escape, before he discovered her situation. But Molly had long realised that she had no hope of that. She had no friends or relatives to take her in, no money of her own, and no ability to save any of the meagre income she earned, due to her husband's greed. She was trapped.

The baby grew slowly. It took several months before even Molly could notice the difference on her malnourished frame, and then it was still simple enough to hide the changes, as long as Richard did not get too close. Molly knew that Richard would inevitably learn the truth, but she feared for what would happen that day, to both her and her child. She lay awake at night, barely able to breathe from fear, wishing she had never met Billy, wishing he had not abandoned her. She felt desperately protective of the child growing inside of her, but she did not know what life she could possibly offer it, or what hope of a future it had. She did not even know if the two of them would survive long enough for the child to emerge into the world.

Torn apart by worry and fear, Molly turned pale, her skin taking on a tone of grey. She often felt weak, worked slowly enough to attract comment, and barely had the energy to speak.

One of her fellow factory girls must have noticed her condition, because someone informed the foreman. Whether the report was made out of concern or malice, Molly did not know. The result was the same either way.

She was asked to leave the factory, and her one potential source of income was lost.

She waited several days to inform Richard. Perhaps, she thought, he would not notice that she was not working, just as he had not noticed her condition. Perhaps he would forget to demand her money, or at least not realise how long it had been since she had last been paid. It was not a strategy that would succeed forever, but, like with the baby, all Molly could think to do was delay the inevitable storm as long as possible, and hope some solution would emerge to allow her and the child to escape relatively unscathed.

But the men gossiped at their work on the docks as much as the women did, and when Richard slammed open the front door of the house one evening, his face almost purple with fury, Molly knew that he knew.

"You!" he spat as he strode across the room toward her. Molly tried to stand, but her legs shook beneath her, and she stumbled. "You lying harlot!"

Molly opened her mouth to defend herself, to defuse the situation, to say *anything*, but no words came out. Her hands instinctively moved to her stomach, covering it protectively, and Richard's eyes narrowed as he followed the movement.

"You're not even going to try to deny it?" he asked. "I suppose there's no point, is there? The truth'll come out soon enough. Perkins *congratulated* me today on my coming child. His wife had heard that you were with child, you see. He heard you were kicked out of the factory because of it. I told him he was mistaken, but he'll check soon enough, won't he? He'll find out it was true, and that I knew nothing about it. You've made a fool out of me, woman!"

He snatched Molly by the wrist. She gasped and tried to pull away, but his grip was too strong.

"Please," she begged. She wanted to plead for the baby, for its need for its mother to be well, but she knew that would only make the situation worse. There was nothing she could say.

"You disgust me," Richard said. He released her wrist with a shove, and she stumbled. Her back collided with the table, and she fell to her knees. "Who was it, hmm? Did he pay you? I can't imagine he paid you well."

Molly shook her head. Tears streamed down her cheeks.

"Get rid of it," he spat. "You hear me? You get rid of it, and you tell everyone they were wrong."

"I can't!" Molly gasped. "Please, I can't."

"You'll find a way," he said.

"No," she said. She clutched her stomach. She could feel the child shifting there, agitated by her pain. This was her *child*. She could not hurt it. "I can't, I can't."

"Do it," he spat, "or I'll do it for you."

Molly scrambled to her feet again, backing up toward the door. She shook her head, one hand held out defensively, the other still clutching her stomach.

"Go on, then!" Richard shouted. "Run. Get out of my sight. But if you even think of coming back here with that brat still in your belly, I'll kill you both myself. You hear me, Molly? You're *mine*. Don't come back until you remember it."

She hesitated in the doorway, reaching for her cloak, and Richard picked up a bottle from the table and hurled it in her direction. Molly screamed and ducked. The bottle exploded into a shower of glass as Richard reached for another.

Molly ran.

CHAPTER SEVEN

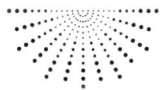

Molly knew that her choices were limited. She had no relatives and no friends. She had no job to bring in an income, and even if someone would hire her in her condition, she would struggle to find somewhere that would pay enough to cover rent for a place of her own. And that was assuming that a landlord was willing to rent to her in the first place. She knew better than anyone that Richard was a cruel and spiteful man, and she had injured his pride. She would not be surprised if he worked his hardest to ensure that no one would support her. He would not skimp on drinking money so that she could eat, but he would certainly be willing to spend more than a little of it on bribes to make her suffer.

She had no hope of gaining domestic work in her condition. No one would accept a single mother as a maid. And she did not dare go to the workhouse. She would be dooming her child to a life of misery if she did.

She spent the first night curled up beneath a bridge, thankful that it at least provided some cover from the drizzling rain. The cold seeped through her thin clothes, settling in her bones. She was too exhausted and despairing to cry or to sleep. She sat up all night, her knees pulled against her chest, rubbing her hands against the cold, desperately, desperately trying to think of some solution to her plight.

No matter how much she thought, it seemed hopeless. Richard would not forgive her, she knew. He would not change his mind. She was on her own. But even if she managed to find food and shelter enough to survive until the baby came… even then, what could she do? The streets were no place for a child. Even if they both survived, what life would the baby have? She wanted her child to feel safe and loved. She wanted them to have a good life. But what could she do? What could she possibly offer them? The child's future was bleak, before it had even been born.

The next morning, Molly swallowed any remaining pride she might have had and returned to the rope factory to beg for her job. With tears in her eyes, she told the foreman that her husband had forsaken her, that she had no money for her child, nothing to eat and nowhere to live. And she was always a hard and dependable worker. Surely he could find it in his heart to help her.

But the foreman seemed to have even less sympathy for her than before. He looked disgusted that her husband had abandoned her but placed the blame firmly with her. It would damage the reputation of the factory, he said, to hire her again. She would be a corrupting influence on the other workers. Best she leave sharpish, he told her, before he contacted the police.

Molly walked from factory to factory after that. Sometimes she tried to hide her condition. Other times, she used her pregnancy as a plea for sympathy. Neither approach worked. No one had a position they were willing to give her. All she had for a day's hard effort was an empty stomach and aching, blistered feet.

Yet she was forced to try it the next day, and the next. She ate what scraps she could scavenge, but soon she was too weak and hungry to continue walking the city. Instead, she resorted to begging for money, hoping that some rich soul would see her belly and take pity on her. Most did not, and some offered her lectures or abuse instead of coin, but she collected a few pennies, enough to feed herself for a little longer.

But she knew that time was running out. The baby was not due for another couple of months, and she needed to eat and rest enough to support both of them until that day. When the baby did come, how would she give birth to it? In the street, alone? She imagined herself bleeding out on the filthy stones, her child dying beside her. She imagined the babe succumbing to hunger, or to cold, alone in the world.

Finally, in desperation, she returned to the midwife who had first confirmed her pregnancy. Molly had no money to pay her for additional assistance, but perhaps she would find it in her heart to take pity on a poor, homeless woman.

For her part, the midwife did not turn her away. She could do little to help her, she said, but she looked moved by Molly's plight.

"At the workhouse, they will take care of both you *and* your baby," she said, but Molly shook her head fiercely.

"There must be some other way," she said. "But my husband will not let me return until the child is gone."

The midwife gave her a sympathetic look. She seemed to consider something for a moment, and then nodded to herself. "If you need the child *gone*," she said slowly, "then I know of a doctor who could help. He will charge you, though."

"Anything," Molly said. "Please."

The midwife gave Molly directions, and Molly thanked her profusely before stepping out onto the street again.

She saw no sense in hesitating. She set out to find it at once. But as she walked, she pressed her hand to her stomach. Her *child*. How could she possibly throw her child away? How could she go on with her life without the baby there?

The doctor's office, if she could call it that, was tucked down a side-alley. The door was unmarked, and no one responded when she first knocked, making her think perhaps she had come to the wrong address. Then a head stuck out of the window above. "What d'ya want?" the older woman shouted.

"I—" Molly's voice shook. She swallowed and tried again. "I wanted to see Doctor Johnson. Is he available?"

The woman above looked Molly up and down, taking in the curve of her stomach and her dishevelled appearance. "Yeah," she said, after a moment. "Wait there."

The window slammed shut, and Molly heard fading footsteps. Another few minutes passed, and then the door creaked open a crack, revealing a tall, elderly man. He wore small glasses on the end of his long, pointed nose. His moustache curled at the ends, and he gave Molly a thin smile as he beckoned her inside.

"I apologise for the delay, miss," he said. He reached around her to close the door behind her. "Please, follow me."

"Are you Doctor Johnson?" Molly asked tentatively as he led her down the corridor. The air had a sickly smell to it, and Molly had to repress her shudder.

"I am," the man said. His voice was silky, almost too quiet to hear. It made goose bumps rise on her skin. "And what might your name be?"

"Do—do you need to know it?" Molly asked.

"Not if you do not wish to give it."

Molly considered for a moment. "My name is Molly," she said eventually. She would be safer if she omitted her surname.

"Molly," he repeated, rolling the word around on his tongue. "And you are here because you have a... *problem*. One you would like me to solve, yes?"

Molly could not speak. Instead, reluctantly, she nodded.

"Very well," Doctor Johnson said.

He led Molly into a small room and gestured at a wooden chair for her to sit. Molly did so, and he settled opposite her, giving her that same oily smile. "Luckily for you, Molly, that is one of my specialties."

Molly still could not speak. The sickly smell was even stronger here than it had been in the corridor. Everything about this place set her nerves on edge. Her instincts screamed at her to leave now and never, never return, to run while she still could, but she would not have come here if she had any other choice. She could not listen to her heart or her conscience now.

"How long have you been in this condition?" Doctor Johnson asked.

"Do—do you mean, on the street, or—"

Doctor Johnson chuckled. "How long have you been with child?"

"About—about seven and a half months," she said. "That means there is about a month and a half to go, doesn't it?"

"Usually, yes," Doctor Johnson said. "But if you need the child gone... well, that will be where I come in." He tilted his head in a mockery of sympathy. "I can remove and dispose of your problem, if you wish it. For a price, of course."

"A—a price," Molly repeated. She had known there would be a fee involved, but the word *price* made it sound far more sinister. "How much?" It hardly mattered what price he named, when she hardly had a penny to call her own, but still, she needed to know. "I don't have much money."

"Ah, I do not do this for the profit," Doctor Johnson said. "I only wish to help. I can perform the procedure for two pounds."

"*Two pounds?*" She had only earned ten pounds a year at the factory. She could not possibly hope to collect so much.

"I wish to help," Doctor Johnson said, "but understand that I act at risk to myself and my own wealth and reputation.

If you had inquired earlier, you might have taken one of many far cheaper concoctions, but now I can only assist you with the knife, and that incurs expenses."

Molly pressed a hand to her stomach again. She did not want to be there. And she did not have two pounds to give him, even if she wanted to.

"Take some time to consider it," Doctor Johnson said. "I am certain you can find the money if you put all your resources behind it. You can trust that I will be here and available when you return."

CHAPTER EIGHT

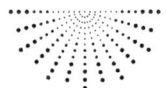

Molly resisted the inevitable for several more days. She desperately tried to think of any other solution to her problem, but there were none. If she continued to carry the child, they would both die. She needed the doctor's help.

It had been three weeks since Richard had turned her out on the street when she knocked on the door of her home again. She held her breath as she heard Richard cross the room inside and then yank open the door.

"You're back, are you?" he grunted. "Have you taken care of that problem?"

"I'm trying," she said. Her voice shook. "But the doctor I found to help wants two pounds to perform the procedure, and I have no money."

"You think I'm going to give you money?" Richard asked. He laughed. "You think I have two pounds to waste on you?"

"It's the only way," she said. "I'll die otherwise."

"Do you expect that I care?"

"Yes," Molly said, sticking up her chin in defiance. "Yes, you care. People will talk if your pregnant wife dies out on the streets, regardless of what you tell them. They will all think less of you."

"They will put the blame where it belongs," he spat.

"They will talk, regardless," she said. "It will cost you far more than two pounds, when people will not drink or game with you, or when your foreman decides not to promote you, because you leave women under your protection, and potentially your own child, out in the cold to die."

His face was turning purple. "So you think I should accept you back? Raise some other man's bastard child?"

"No," she said, her voice only shaking slightly. "I know you will not. If you pay the doctor, then I—I can return. You can tell everyone they were mistaken, and there was no child, as you wanted. Or you can cast me out, if you wish. But you will be safe."

He considered her for a long moment. She could see the cogs working in his head. Of course, her plan relied on him having two pounds to give. Yet, despite how much he gamed and how little she had always had to eat, she thought he had some winnings stashed away for future use, even if that future use was originally intended to be further gambling.

"What is the name of this doctor?" he asked. "Where can I find him?"

"Doctor Johnson," Molly said. She described the location of his surgery.

"Don't return here until it is dealt with," he said, and he slammed the door in her face.

When Molly returned to Doctor Johnson two days later, she did not truly know what to expect. Had Richard contacted him and paid for the procedure, or would the doctor demand a different kind of payment for his assistance? He might even lie about receiving money from Richard in order to receive more for his work. But Molly was desperate. She could not continue like this.

Doctor Johnson gave her the same oily smile as he welcomed her inside. "Molly," he said. "I am glad to see you've returned. I heard from your husband yesterday. It seems he is as eager for a resolution to this as you are."

"Did he pay you?" Molly asked, unable to keep the desperation from her voice.

Doctor Johnson nodded his head.

"Then—then everything is ready?" she asked. Her voice shook. She put her hand to her stomach. She felt nauseous. She did not wish to lose this baby. But this was the only way. The *only* way.

"Certainly," Doctor Johnson said. "We can begin whenever you wish. Now, if you would like."

Molly forced herself to swallow her fear. "Yes," she said. "Now. Please."

The process was agony. Despite demanding two pounds for the apparently surgical nature of his intervention, Doctor Johnson initially just gave Molly a foul-tasting concoction to drink, before "encouraging" the process with a few terrifying looking tools. Molly thought her screams must have been audible all throughout the city.

It took hours. Molly was drenched with sweat, the agony wracking through her body. She could feel the dampness of blood down her legs. She had never felt more alone in the world. After the doctor's initial intervention, he had left her lying on a bed in this room alone. The two pounds had bought little actual doctoring.

But then, when Molly thought that she could not endure another moment, her body gave a great push, and she heard the baby cry.

Gasping for air, tears rolling down her face, Molly reached for the infant. It was a girl, Molly saw, and she was perfect. Ten tiny fingers and ten tiny toes, bright blue eyes surrounded by tiny eyelashes, a small tuft of hair on her head. Molly reached for a scrap of unstained cloth to wrap her in and then held her tightly to her chest.

This was the only moment they would have, Molly knew. She could not keep the child. She hoped that her husband would never even learn that it had lived. If she had remained pregnant any longer, she knew they both would have died. This had been the child's best chance at living. Molly might wreck her own body, maybe even lose her own life, paying a doctor to have the birth occur early, but the child would have a chance. The midwife had promised that she would take the baby and find her a family that would love her. Molly had no choice but to trust her.

She had known it would be difficult. But now that her daughter was in her arms, she did not know how she would ever force herself to let go. Could they not try, she thought? God, in his mercy, would provide for them. There had to be a way.

But even as Molly thought it, as she clutched the baby tight against her chest, she knew that it would not be. She could still feel the blood escaping her body. Her head felt light, her thoughts unclear, and her body did not feel like her own. She sensed that she was not likely to survive long. If she tried to keep the child, it would still lose her, and she might miss the chance for a better life that the midwife was promising.

Molly held the child as tightly as she could, knowing she would soon have to say goodbye.

The door to the room burst open, and Molly looked up, expecting to see the doctor returning.

Richard was striding toward her, his face set in determination.

She struggled to sit up, still clutching her daughter. "What are you doing here?" she asked.

"Ensuring you don't pull any tricks," he said. "You think the doctor didn't tell me exactly what you were paying him for? I know you told him not to kill the child."

"But she'll be gone," Molly said. "She won't be in your life. No one will know where she came from."

Richard did not listen. He wrenched the baby from Molly's arms. She screamed in helpless desperation, but Richard was already striding away.

Doctor Johnson stood by the doorway, watching impassively.

Molly stumbled to her feet as Richard disappeared from the room. Her hair was stuck to her face with sweat, and her nightgown was stained through with blood. She had no shoes and no coat, and she was so dizzy from the blood loss that she could barely stand, but she stumbled after her husband as fast as she could.

He was already halfway down the street by the time she stepped outside. "No!" she cried after him. "Richard, stop!"

Richard ignored her. A passer-by looked over at them, but one look at the scene sent him hurrying quickly away.

"No," Molly gasped again. She needed to catch up with him, she *had* to save her baby, but her legs would not move fast enough. She staggered, and just caught herself against the wall before she fell. "You can't," she begged.

Richard disappeared around the corner, and Molly stumbled after him. When she next saw him again, she gasped. He was striding straight towards the river.

"Please," she said, but no one listened to her. She fell to her knees, weak and desperate from lack of blood, as Richard reached the bank. Without looking back, he hurled the child into the water, and Molly screamed.

CHAPTER NINE

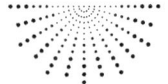

Further down the river, Jeremiah Wentworth was having an unremarkable day.

Jeremiah had recently turned sixty, but advanced age was no reason to stop working, and he still laboured as hard as he could every day as a fisherman. He and his wife Elizabeth had been married for almost forty years, but they had never been blessed with living children. His Lizzie did laundry in the neighbourhood, and that, combined with the income he earned from his fish, was enough for both of them to live in simple comfort.

He had been out on the sea since before dawn, pulling in an average catch and selling it on, but now it was the middle of the afternoon, and he was taking the long route home. It was Lizzie's fifty-eighth birthday, that very day, and he intended to collect some flowers for her. A few pretty varieties grew by the riverside; weeds, technically, so no one would argue with him picking them, but lovely enough to brighten their home for a few days. He hoped he might pass a market stall later, once he stepped away from the river, and find a trinket or two as well.

He whistled as he walked, content in his own company. Sometimes, young couples walked along the side of this river. The larger one on the other side of the city stank of pollution, but this one lay a little outside the denser parts of Liverpool, shaded by trees. It was a peaceful place. But today, Jeremiah walked alone.

He walked closer to the water's edge and watched the ducks bobbing on the surface, and then turned to the bank, where the flowers grew. His attention was caught by a flash of red, and he paused. There was a small bundle of red and white, resting half on the riverbank and half in the water. It began to drift idly downstream again, and Jeremiah stepped forward, stopping its movement with his foot.

When he realised what he was looking at, he almost shouted in surprise. It was a bundle of rough cloth, stained with blood, and whatever was wrapped inside it was moving.

Dreading what he would see but knowing he could not leave a potentially injured creature unaided, he reached down, ignoring the pain in his back, and picked up the bundle. He pulled back the cloth to reveal the pale face of a sleeping baby. Sleeping, or unconscious, he thought. Not dead, though. The child was still moving.

Jeremiah was not a fool. He understood how the world worked, after sixty years of experience. He saw at once that the baby had not fallen in the river by accident. Someone had tossed the child away.

He quickly pulled the rest of the cloth away, looking for the baby's injuries. But the child seemed unharmed. Her breathing was perhaps a little slow from being in the cold water, but Jeremiah was no doctor, so he could not be certain. But she had no wounds. She was not bleeding. She was absolutely tiny, much smaller than Jeremiah's own children had been in the days between their births and deaths, but she was perfectly formed and whole.

The blood had been someone else's, then. Perhaps the mother's.

The babe looked as though it had barely been in the world for a day, yet it was clear that it had experienced tragedy.

The baby stirred and began to cry. That, Jeremiah thought, was a good sign. If the baby was weak, it would not cry. He removed the rest of the cloth and shrugged off his coat, wrapping the child up in it as snugly as he could.

An orphan, or at least an unwanted babe. What was he to do with it? He could not leave it here.

Sense would tell him to take the child to the church or a private orphanage. They would care for her. But as the babe shifted in his arms, settling down again, he found that he did not wish to let the child go.

God had provided for her, after all. He had protected her when she mostly likely should have drowned and brought her tiny bundle to Jeremiah's feet. Jeremiah knew his Bible. He had known the story of Moses since he was small. This babe was no prophet, he thought with a smile, but she had been blessed by God, and He had blessed Jeremiah, too, by choosing him to receive her.

Jeremiah and Lizzie were far too old to have their own children now. It had been twenty-five years since the last one had been born sleeping, and the couple had long since accepted that a family was not in the plan for them. But as Jeremiah held the baby in his arms, he thought that perhaps the plan had merely been different from what he expected.

This babe had come into his care. If his wife agreed—and, he felt, she certainly would, for she had the biggest heart of anyone he knew—then the babe would join their family and grow with them.

He walked quickly home after that, the flowers forgotten. When he stepped inside, he immediately saw Lizzie in the kitchen, cooking something on the hearth.

His wife had always been an unusual beauty. Her loose and broad shoulders were not, he thought, what a nobleman would have considered classically lovely, but those men knew nothing about such things. They wanted a wife who could barely stand against a strong breeze. Lizzie had the look of a woman who could take care of herself, and that self-assurance was what had first attracted Jeremiah's attention. She was striking to look at, impossible to turn away from, and she never shied away from the attention. She could have been an army general, Jeremiah sometimes thought, if not for her kindness and her sex. She had that ability to command people, and to get things done. She was older now, her hair more grey than brown, her smile lines long since become true wrinkles, but she was just as beautiful, Jeremiah thought, as the day he first met her. More beautiful, in fact, because as he looked at her face now, he saw all their years together.

"You're back late," Lizzie said, without turning to look at him. "I heard from Dennis that you packed up for the day a couple of hours ago. Where've you been?"

"I was looking for something for your birthday," Jeremiah said slowly, "but—"

"Oh, psh," Lizzie said. "You silly man. What use do I have for birthdays at my age?" She turned around, and then stopped, mouth agape, as she looked at the bundle in her husband's arms. "Jeremiah Wentworth," she said. "What in the name of Heaven is that?" She marched forward without waiting for an answer. "A *baby*?" she gasped. "Jeremiah, where on earth did she come from?"

"I found her," Jeremiah said simply, "floating in the river."

"In the *river*?" Lizzie reached out and took the baby in her arms. "Oh, you poor darling," she said, when she pulled back the coat and revealed the girl's face. "She's a tiny thing. How is she alive?"

"Grace," Jeremiah said. "It was a miracle that I saw her. It was a miracle she was still alive when I did."

"She will be hungry soon enough," Lizzie said. "I'll take her across the street to Mrs Lewis's. She just had a little boy of her own. She might have some milk to spare. You don't think her mother is looking for her?"

"I don't think so," Jeremiah said. He took off his hat and placed it sadly on the table. "I think she's alone in the world."

"Poor mite," Lizzie said. She rocked the girl in her arms. "I'll get her to Mrs Lewis. It won't be a long-term solution, but it'll hold her over. My sister told me that goat's milk is better than cow's, if a mother's milk doesn't come in. Or that new condensed milk they've been selling at the store. I heard that's a good choice for babies. I'll have to ask Mrs Lewis if she knows anything while I'm there."

She strode off with the babe before Jeremiah could reply. He had not even had the chance to mention the idea of keeping the child, but that did not seem to matter. Lizzie, it seemed, had made up her mind as soon as she saw the babe, so firmly that she did not even consider it worth mentioning aloud.

The babe would remain with them now.

CHAPTER TEN

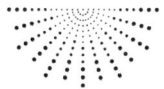

Jeremiah and Lizzie named the baby Dora, after Lizzie's late mother. It might have been wise, Jeremiah thought later, not to get too attached to the child. They had first-hand experience of how easy it was for a babe to die, and Dora was more likely to be fragile than most, considering how tiny she was and how Jeremiah had discovered her. It was asking for heartbreak to fall in love so quickly. But Lizzie and Jeremiah both had large hearts with ample space for love, and the early loss of all their own children had left a hole that they ached to fill, even after so many years. One look at the tiny girl with her bright blue eyes, and they both fell.

Luckily, the tiny mite had a fierce will to live. She drank the milk that Lizzie gave her greedily, and although she remained very small for her age, she began to grow. She learned to crawl, and then to walk, and was soon terrorising Lizzie both inside and outside the house. She was slow to speak, but once she did, all the words seemed to flow out of her at once, and the once-silent child seemed to become physically unable to be quiet or still. And although Lizzie and Jeremiah could not indulge her with toys and treats the way rich parents might, they adored their miracle girl, and doted upon her in a way that stricter parents might consider foolish.

Dora was as full of questions as she was of energy, and she always wanted to know not only the *what* but also the *why* of everything she saw. Her hair grew into a mass of wispy brown curls that no comb could tame, and her round cheeks were always rosy with joy and exertion. Although her start in this life had been perilous, she showed little sign of it as she grew.

The only cause for concern—and it was a minor one, Lizzie and Jeremiah always thought—was that her parents were not as young as parents tended to be. They were aged more like doting grandparents than those directly responsible for raising a toddler, and sometimes they struggled to keep up with her boundless energy. Jeremiah also worried what would happen to the girl when they passed on. He and Lizzie were both healthy for their age, but by the time Dora turned three, Lizzie was sixty-one and he was sixty-three. The sea breeze chilled his bones far more than it ever used to do, and his legs always ached whenever it rained. They might yet live another thirty years, long enough to see Dora grown and settled and possibly with children of her own. But that was unlikely, compared to the possibility of at least one of them dying within ten. Who would care for Dora then? Widows without grown children struggled to support themselves under the best of circumstances. Would Lizzie be able to manage Dora on her own, if Jeremiah died before her? Would Jeremiah cope, if his wife departed before him?

Jeremiah tried not to dwell on such dark thoughts. They had enough money for food and clothes and rent, and for a few small occasional treats besides, but they did not have enough to truly save for future disaster. Besides, the future had always proved difficult to predict. Worry would do more harm than good, when they could do nothing to change the future either way.

Lizzie worried too, although more about Jeremiah than herself. Fishing was hard and potentially dangerous work, and her husband was not as young as he had once been. He moved slower and could carry less weight, and although Lizzie would never mention it, she worried that Jeremiah would get seriously hurt one day. But fishing paid well. It was a better job than working in a factory, for both health and compensation. And the couple had no savings. Jeremiah needed to work for them all to live.

Sometimes, Lizzie wondered what had happened to Dora's parents. Had she truly been unwanted, or had some tragedy occurred that day that tore her away from a mother who had loved her? Lizzie knew she would probably never be certain. All she could do was provide the best possible life for Dora in her original mother's stead.

Until one day, three years after Dora first came into their lives, Jeremiah was late returning from work. He still went out onto the sea every day, hauling in whatever catch he could, and the early morning nature of the work meant he was usually home fairly early in the evening too, but even as Lizzie finished up dinner and fed Dora, her husband did not appear. She put Dora to bed, but she could not settle herself, fearing that something terrible had occurred.

The news, when it came, was better than she had feared, but far worse than she had hoped. Two men carried Jeremiah into the house around midnight. Jeremiah was clearly breathing but unconscious, and his right arm was gone.

Lizzie pressed a hand over her open mouth as she hurried to her husband's side. The men who had brought him home told her the news in low, serious voices. There had been an accident, they told her, and his arm had become trapped. The doctor said it could not be saved. The man acted quickly, they said, and he knocked Jeremiah out with some strong-smelling concoction from his bag, but it was uncertain how long Jeremiah would sleep now, but it was guaranteed that the pain would be difficult to bear when he finally awoke.

Dora slept through the entire affair, and Lizzie was grateful for it. When she did wake, the following morning, she was distressed by both Jeremiah's condition and Lizzie's own fears, and she cried noisily by her father's bedside, clinging to Lizzie whenever she could.

Lizzie wrapped an arm around her too, but her mind was elsewhere. It was with the rent that still needed paying every week, and the cupboards that would soon run bare without income. Her husband could not fish with only one arm. A younger man, perhaps, could have adapted to the change, but Jeremiah was over sixty, with an aching back and far slower movements than he had in his youth. If he went out on the boat with only one arm, he would struggle at best, and probably find himself in serious danger, unable to respond quickly to the changing moods of the sea. The doctor who amputated his arm also required paying, and although Lizzie did laundry and mending when she could, it was not enough to cover all those fees.

She worried for herself and Jeremiah, but they had already lived good lives, and they were used to tragedy and changing circumstances. Her greatest fear was for Dora. The child was only three, and Lizzie knew in her heart that her duty to the girl was to ensure she had the best life she possibly could. How could the child have a good life with an elderly couple with no work, one who might soon end up in the workhouse or on the streets?

Lizzie feared the workhouse for herself and her husband. She had heard stories of families separated, husbands and wives never able to see one another, and of how the place trapped you and exhausted you so you could never get back on your feet and leave again. But what would that mean for little Dora, growing up there? How could Lizzie and Jeremiah keep a child that they could not afford to feed or house?

When Jeremiah's thoughts were more coherent, and Dora was asleep, Lizzie raised the issue with her husband. "Perhaps it is selfish," she said softly, "to keep her, if we cannot provide for her?"

"But who else will provide for her?" Jeremiah asked. "She has no one else."

"The church," Lizzie said. "They have an orphanage. She would be well cared for there."

"An orphanage?" Jeremiah repeated. "But she would be alone. We couldn't guarantee she was kept safe."

"The Lord has looked out for her so far," Lizzie said. "An orphanage run in the name of the Lord will be able to protect her. But I fear what will happen if she remains with us. If she grows too old for the orphanage to be willing to find space for her. I hear terrible stories of the children in the workhouse, the violence that they face, almost never able to see their parents. How could we forgive ourselves, if we tried to keep her and she ended up there? Or if she ended up on the street? We will struggle to even feed ourselves. We can't cling to her, when she's better off elsewhere."

"You're right, my dear," Jeremiah said. "As always, you are right. I only wish there was another option."

And so, a few days later, they bundled up all of Dora's possessions and dropped her off at the church orphanage's door.

CHAPTER ELEVEN

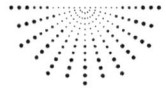

Dora did not hear the conversation that passed between Jeremiah and Lizzie, and she did not understand that they could not feed and house her now, no matter how much they wished to, despite being able to before. She was only three years old, and so despite Lizzie and Jeremiah's promises that they loved her and that she was going to good people to have the best possible life, she felt deep in her heart that she had been abandoned by the only family she had ever known.

She remained quiet when they first left her at the orphanage, as they had bid her to be, but as time passed and she began to realise that her parents would not return, she began to cry.

No one comforted her. The orphanage was run with the best of intentions, but the truth was that there were far more orphans than the number of orphanage volunteers could reasonably care for. They worked hard to ensure that all the children were adequately fed and clothed, and that they had a roof to sleep under every night, but they did not have the time to care for each child's less obvious needs. The children were generally left to their own devices when not in school, and nobody noticed Dora crying when four other young children had arrived the same day as her, and one was currently tearing up the dormitory. Little Dora was almost invisible. The only people who noticed her were other children, and they mocked her for being a crybaby.

Dora's only comfort was the cloth doll that she brought to the orphanage with her. There might have been a risk of it being stolen at such a place, but Dora clung so tightly to it that not even superhuman strength could have pried her fingers off her dolly's arm.

No matter how much Dora cried, Lizzie and Jeremiah did not come back. She began to wonder what she had done wrong to cause them to send her away, and desperately tried to think of what she could do to make them return for her again. Perhaps, she thought, there was something wrong with her, deep down in her heart, that led them to leave her here. All she could think of to bring them back was to be as good as she possibly could. And so, the once-lively and boisterous toddler became quiet and withdrawn, hoping that if she followed every instruction and never inspired a harsh word, her parents would return.

This only served to make her more invisible to those in charge of the orphanage. Children who kicked and screamed were punished, yes, but they were also noticed, and although none of the children could possibly receive all of the care and attention they needed, those who grabbed their carers' attention undeniably received more of it. A child who made their pain and suffering known had a chance of one of the carers taking particular interest in them. Dora suffered in silence, and so the overstressed, overworked volunteers did not notice her pain.

Dora had never been hungry with Jeremiah and Lizzie, but she was hungry now. The orphanage relied on donations to buy food, and although it did have some wealthy and generous patrons, there were many children to feed, and many other costs to cover. Dora quickly became accustomed to eating gruel for most meals of the day, and even that needed to be guarded as fiercely as she guarded her dolly, lest one of the older children try to steal her portion.

The orphanage was cold, too, without the money to light fires in most of the rooms, and only one blanket given to each child. Dora spent her first winter there shivering at night beneath the thin woollen cloth, squeezed next to two or three other small girls for warmth.

It was not all darkness, however. Although some of the other children were bullies, and others were too shy to talk, Dora began to make friends among the other girls around her age. Five-year-old Catherine Hall, known as

Cat, had been at the orphanage since she was born, so she knew exactly how everything worked. She knew the warmest nooks and crannies to hide in, and who might be convinced to hand out an extra ladle of gruel. Some children would have taken this knowledge and used it for power over others, but Cat was not that sort of girl. She took Dora under her wing, and although she found it strange how Dora refused to get up to even the mildest of mischief, she found she liked this strange newcomer.

Dora still felt deeply lonely without Jeremiah and Lizzie, and dreamed constantly of the day that they would return to fetch her. But at least she was not alone.

Three years passed at the orphanage. Every morning, Dora would wake up in the crowded dormitory and pray that *today* would be the day that her parents would come back for her. Every night, she knelt by her bedside and prayed to God that *tomorrow* would be the day. More than anything, Dora wanted a family.

So, when Mrs Lucas, one of the more important adults who ran the orphanage, called Dora into her study, Dora had to fight the urge to run all the way there. She was certain that her prayers had finally been answered, and that Lizzie and Jeremiah were waiting for her, ready to take her home.

She did not run. A good child would not run, and she would not allow herself to do anything that might lead them to leave again without her. She walked silently into the study, but she looked about for her parents' faces.

"Ah, here is the child now," Mrs Lucas said to two adults sitting in chairs, facing away from the door. They both turned to look, and Dora had to fight back her cry of dismay. They were not her parents. She did not recognise either of them.

They were both in their mid-forties, although Dora was not a good judge of that. The woman had a long, thin face with a pointed chin. The man had a round face, and he was balding slightly on top.

"Dora Wentworth," Mrs Lucas said. "She has been with us for three years. Six years old."

"She's skinny," the woman said. Her voice was low and a little raspy.

Mrs Lucas nodded, as though conceding the point. "We do not have the funds to feed the children as much as we might like," she said. "But the child is strong. Obedient. She is quiet, without being insufferably shy. I think she would suit you quite well."

Dora looked up at the two strangers, waiting for them to speak. They turned back to Mrs Lucas without addressing Dora at all. "Yes," the woman said. "She will do fine. She has no ailments, does she? No expensive issues?"

"No, no," Mrs Lucas said. "Not at all. Dora," she added, "this is Mr and Mrs Brown. This lovely couple are looking for a daughter, and they have selected you. They are to be your new parents."

"I already have parents!" Dora said quickly.

"Dora came to us a little older than many," Mrs Lucas said to Mr and Mrs Brown. "For the first years of her life, she was cared for by an older couple who found her soon after she was born. But they stopped being able to care for her, and so they thought it best if they brought her here. But I can assure you, they gave up all rights to her. She is available for adoption."

Dora shook her head. She could feel tears stinging in her eyes, but she blinked them back. Good girls did not cry. Her parents would not come back for her if she cried. "They'll come back," she said.

"If the girl is simple—" Mrs Brown began, but Mrs Lucas shook her head, interrupting her.

"No, no," she said, "not simple. Young, a little naive perhaps, but smart enough. Change can be difficult for all of the children, after the routine they've enjoyed here. But they all adapt quickly enough."

"Very well," Mr Brown said. "Let us get the business over with. What do we need to sign? We'll take the child with us now."

"Immediately?" Mrs Lucas asked. She sounded surprised, but she did not argue. "That is good of you," she said. "We need all the spare beds we can get."

Dora frowned at them, trying to understand. "I'm leaving?" she asked.

"Yes, girl," Mrs Brown said. She stood up. She was surprisingly tall, and she looked down at Dora without any softness or kindness in her eyes. "Go and fetch your things."

"Ah," Mrs Lucas said. She stood, too. "All the children's possessions are property of the orphanage. She may wear her clothes, of course, but we require everything else for the other children."

"Very well," Mrs Brown said, although she sounded annoyed. Dora, however, shook her head. She could not leave everything behind.

"But my dolly," she said. "Can I take Dolly with me?"

"What do you want with a worthless doll, child?" Mrs Brown asked.

"Please," Dora asked. "My mama made her for me."

"Fine, yes," Mrs Lucas said, with a dismissive wave of her hand. "Take that if you wish. Go and fetch it now, girl, and say your goodbyes. The grownups have a little more to discuss."

Dora curtsied automatically and walked out of the room in a daze. She knew what adoption meant. A few of the other children had left the orphanage in the same way over the three years that she had been there. Usually, babies were the ones who got adopted, while older boys might be taken on as assistances or apprentices. But Mr and Mrs Brown wished for a child Dora's age, and Dora had been the one that Mrs Lucas had chosen.

Dora knew she should feel grateful. She had dreamed of having a real family again, and even though Mr and Mrs Brown were not her parents, they had to be good and generous people, to want to take an unwanted child like Dora into their lives. They frightened her a little, but that was because they were strangers. Maybe she would even grow to see them as her parents in time.

But Dora did not want that. She wanted Jeremiah and Lizzie to return for her. She wanted to have finally been good enough for them to love her again.

She collected her dolly from her bed and walked slowly back to Mrs Lucas's office, clutching Dolly to her chest. The other children were all attending school, so she did not see them. She could not even say goodbye to Cat.

Mr and Mrs Brown ordered her to follow them, and she had no choice but to obey.

CHAPTER TWELVE

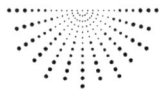

Maude and Clifford Brown were not naturally the parental type. They ran a tavern of the sort that Richard Wilkins had once been a common patron to, and their greatest concerns were making a profit and being popular with their customers, in that order. They cut corners when they could, scammed when they couldn't, and greeted everyone who arrived at the tavern with a smile and a joke as though they were long-lost family, before robbing them behind their backs.

Maude and Clifford did not have any children of their own, and they would not have found this disappointing, if not for the sheer amount of work that running a tavern required. Drinks had to be served and meals cooked, bedsheets changed and laundry done, and no trickery could erase these tasks entirely, at least if they wanted any guests to stay.

The Bull and Sow, as their tavern was called, could not have been described as savoury by even the most generous assessor, and it was certainly not a suitable place for a child.

Unfortunately, the workers at the orphanage did not know this, and they probably could not have acted upon the knowledge, even if they had it. The volunteers at the orphanage were overworked, with far more children to care for than they had either time or money for. If a couple arrived at the orphanage looking for a child, and they had an address and some apparent form of income, then they were almost inevitably given a child, to make space at the orphanage for the others in need. And once a child was adopted, the orphanage did not have the time or the resources to check on the children again. They relied on the charity and decency of those who took children in, and unfortunately, such charity and decency were not always ensured.

If Maude and Clifford Brown had been known criminals, things might have been different. But as far as the justice system was concerned, they were upstanding citizens who now wished to take in a needy child as their own, and nothing was likely to stop them.

It probably does not need to be said that the Browns were not truly interested in having a daughter. They did not wish for a child to love, or to help one in need. They wanted a worker who they would not have to pay, a child young enough to be malleable but old enough to be useful.

A girl, they had decided, as the work was mostly domestic, and girls were more easily brought into hand either way. A quiet and obedient one, who would not cause them any trouble.

Dora's desperate attempt to be good enough for her parents to return had made her the perfect candidate.

Of course, if you asked Mr and Mrs Brown, they would not have thought they were being cruel, and many people would have agreed with them. They planned to feed Dora and give her a room of her own, which was far more than she had at the orphanage. She would no longer benefit from the schooling that the church provided, but she did not need to care for herself or look for work outside what the family would now provide her, so that seemed rather irrelevant. Many children received no schooling. The important thing was that she would have a home. Love and affection did not come into it.

Dora scurried behind Mr and Mrs Brown as they led her through the streets toward her new home. The Bull and Sow was a thin, rickety-looking building on a narrow, winding street, not far from the docks. Even in the bright sunshine of midday, the street had a murky feeling to it, with shadows cast by the several-story buildings huddling close on either side.

Some patrons were already drinking when Mr and Mrs Brown led Molly inside. They hurried her past the tables and behind the bar, where an uneven wooden staircase led upstairs.

"You'll sleep in the attic room," Mrs Brown said as she hurried Dora along. "You'll be up first, caring for the fires and the like. Your job is to do what you're told, when you're told it, and to keep our guests happy. You can manage a simple thing like that, now, can't you?"

Dora nodded.

The work turned out to be both hard and endless. Dora was still only six years old, and she was small and weak for her age after years of malnutrition, but the Browns worked her as though she were a fully grown, full-time maid. Dora was the one who cleaned the pub and all the rooms at the inn. She changed the bedsheets, crushing any lice she found with her fingers as she worked. She scrubbed the floors, and wiped the smog from the windows, and even helped in the kitchen when Mrs Brown demanded it. She never spoke to any of the customers, always keeping her head down and moving as quickly as she could, and they rarely tried to speak to her, but she often heard them speaking *about* her, as though she could not hear. They laughed at her scrawny arms and legs, and asked Mr and Mrs Brown where they could find a thing like her for themselves.

"At the orphanage!" Mrs Brown replied with a laugh, and the customers laughed too.

Dora tried her hardest to count her blessings. She had a roof over her head, a bed all of her own, and was better fed than she had been at the orphanage. Yes, she was often punished—for working too slow or being too clumsy—with the loss of supper, and yes, sometimes the Browns forgot to feed her altogether, forcing her to grab what scraps from the kitchen she could find, but the food was there. The house was warm.

And if her mama and papa wanted her again, they could find her here, couldn't they? The orphanage would tell them where she had gone if they returned. So, the best thing she could do was remain here and be as quiet and good as she could.

Dora did not allow herself to cry. She didn't cry after spending the entire day scrubbing the sticky residue of ale off the floor of the pub, and then being told that she had not worked quickly enough and being refused any supper for her aching stomach. She did not cry when she dropped a plate of food, swaying with exhaustion, and Mrs Brown hit her around the face in retribution. She did not cry when the patrons of the inn mocked her or teased her, or when they grabbed at her wrist as she passed them, seizing her attention to make more demands.

She did not even cry when she was ten years old, and the Browns decided that she was not doing enough to earn her keep. She was old enough now, they decided, to serve drinks and meals in the pub itself, and so what little free time and sleep Dora managed to scrape was now taken over by evenings spent in the pub's crowded hall, squeezing past intoxicated patrons and trying to ignore their shouted comments.

By age twelve, Dora was covered in bruises and scars from the "correction" of her guardians. She swayed on her feet from exhaustion, and worst of all, she began to notice that some of the male patrons' gazes lingered on her longer, the more that she grew. She dreaded squeezing her way through the crowded pub, knowing she might be forced to brush against a patron and endure their leering smiles as she did.

Dora had accepted that her mother and father were not coming back for her. She was much older now, wiser in the world, and she fully understood now that they had not really been her parents. They had taken her in out of charity, and the world had not rewarded them for their generosity. She could not expect them to continue to care for an orphan like her, when she was not even truly their relation, when she could provide them no support and was more trouble than she was worth. She was lucky, she thought, that they had chosen to take her to the orphanage, and not simply pushed her out onto the street.

In her head, she accepted this. It was, she knew, the truth. But still Dora longed to be loved. She longed for kindness and affection. She knew she did not deserve it, yet she longed for it, nonetheless.

She would not find it at the Bull and Sow. But Dora knew that the Browns offered other things that she needed, no matter how terribly they treated her. If she ran away, she would remain alone, and she would soon be starving, too. Besides, she did not want to imagine what Mr Brown would do to her if she tried to escape and was caught. So, she stayed, and she worked, never earning a penny, never getting any closer to freedom, but always dreaming that one day, somehow, it would come.

CHAPTER THIRTEEN

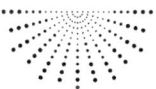

Dora spent ten years working at The Bull and Sow, dreaming of a better life. Although Mr and Mrs Brown—or Uncle Clifford and Aunt Maude, as they insisted she call them—never paid her a penny, and she was now technically old enough to try and make her way in the world herself, her so-called family still provided something like safety and security against the cruelty of the outside world.

At sixteen, Dora remained slight, with long arms and legs. Her wild brown hair had grown into long curls, and her large blue eyes were ringed with thick eyelashes. Her face still had some of the roundness of youth, and her cheeks were always bright and rosy, despite the hardships that she faced. She was a quiet and polite young woman, well practiced at dancing out of the way of wandering hands while carrying drinks through the pub and at hiding the bruises given to her by her aunt and uncle beneath carefully draped clothes and hair.

Dora was not a fool. She had noticed that more and more patrons were paying attention to her, and they were getting less and less subtle about it. They called her *sweetheart* and shouted out compliments at her as she passed, their hands "accidentally" brushing against her. They frightened Dora, but she knew that her aunt and uncle relied on her hard work at the inn and did not think they would allow anyone else to hurt her. It was one thing for them to beat her, as punishment or motivation. It would be quite another for a stranger to harm her, when she belonged to them.

Still, Dora worked hard to ensure that she was never alone with any of the more worrying patrons.

One autumn night, however, one patron simply refused to leave. Uncle Clifford was out, doing who knew what, and Aunt Maude had already retired to bed. The clock on the wall said it was two in the morning, but the man continued to sit at the bar, ordering drink after drink.

"We're closing soon," Dora finally said to him, not looking him in the eye, but he just snorted.

"I'll leave when I'm ready to leave," he said.

He was more neatly dressed than many of their patrons, although several hours at the bar had led him to open the neck of his shirt and loosen his cravat. His hair stuck up from where he had been running his fingers through it, and his chin was dark with stubble, but his clothes were made from good-quality material, and he carried himself like a man who could not doubt his own importance or influence.

Dora did not argue. Eventually, Uncle Clifford would return, and he would ensure the lingering customer left—even if he also blamed Dora for not getting rid of him sooner. If she argued, however, the customer might complain to Uncle Clifford, and then she would be punished for driving money away. Instead, Dora nodded, and distracted herself with cleaning the surface of the bar.

As she worked, she sensed the customer watching her. His eyes lingered on her long limbs, leering as she bent over to work, following her every movement.

She needed to escape his gaze. She was not meant to leave the inn unwatched while customers were inside, but her skin crawled under the man's gaze, and she scurried to the storeroom that led off the back of the tavern.

Dora left the door ajar behind her, and leaned forward against the shelves, struggling to catch her breath. When would Uncle Clifford return home? The customer's looks made her skin crawl, and she did not know how to drive him off by herself. Should she speak more sternly to him, shout at him, perhaps? Or would that just goad him on?

The door creaked behind her, and Dora jumped and turned around. The man was stepping through the doorway, his wide frame blocking any hope of escape.

"I'm sorry, sir," Dora said. Her voice squeaked. "Customers are not allowed in here."

"That's all right," the man said. He stepped closer, pushing the door to behind him. "You'll make an exception for me, now, won't you?"

"Sir," Dora said again. She tried to step around him, but he moved with her, herding her backward against the shelves. "Please, let me go."

"It's just you and me, now, sweetheart, isn't it?" he said. He leaned closer. Dora could smell the alcohol on his hot, heavy breath. He reached forward and brushed her chin with one calloused hand. "We can have some fun, can't we?"

"Don't touch me," Dora breathed. She shoved against him, trying to create enough space to squeeze past, but the man caught her wrists and squeezed tightly, holding her in place.

"Now, don't be like that," he said. He pressed his face even closer. His breath hit Dora's face, and she flinched. He released one of her wrists, moving his hand toward her hip.

Dora slapped him as hard as she could. The man shouted in surprise, and then his grip on her tightened as he surged forward. "You little witch," he shouted. "I'll show you."

"What's going on?" Uncle Clifford's voice rang from the hall.

The man released Dora immediately, and she shoved past him, stumbling out of the store cupboard. Uncle Clifford stood near the bar, his face red with fury.

"What on earth do you think you are doing, girl?" he said, as the man strode out behind her. Dora waited for him to confront the customer too, but Uncle Clifford kept his eyes on her as the man threw a wink her way, collected his jacket, and strode toward the door.

"Well?" Uncle Clifford asked, as the door clicked shut behind the customer. "Explain yourself, girl."

"Please," Dora said. She felt tears stinging her eyes, and she blinked them back. Crying would not endear her to her uncle at all. It would only make him less likely to sympathise with her or believe her. "That man—he refused to leave. He followed me into the storeroom, and he grabbed me. He tried—"

"You disgust me," Uncle Clifford spat. "We take you in, and raise you, and this is how you behave?"

"Please," Dora said. "I didn't want any of that. Thank you for coming back when you did. Otherwise, I don't—I don't know what might have happened."

"I do," Uncle Clifford said. "And what a waste that would've been. Do you know how many of our customers ask after you, girl? I protect you. And you're just giving it away for free?"

"No!" Dora cried. "He cornered me. He was going to attack me. Please believe me."

Uncle Clifford moved to strike her, and Dora flinched back, scrambling away.

"Harlot!" he said. "This is how you repay us? Get out of my sight."

Dora did not need to be told twice. She turned and ran up the stairs. She could hear Uncle Clifford mumbling to himself and swearing after her, but he did not follow her.

Once she was in the safety of her room, Dora leaned against the door, closed her eyes, and took a long, calming breath. Of course, Uncle Clifford had not believed her. The important thing was that she had escaped relatively unharmed. Nothing had happened to her. And if this inspired her aunt and uncle to watch her more closely, that could only be a good thing. She did not want to risk this ever happening again.

Her wrists ached. She looked down at them to find finger-shaped bruises marring her skin.

A tear ran down her cheek, unbidden. She wiped it away furiously. She would not cry. She would not show weakness now. But if Uncle Clifford had not returned when he had… what would have happened to her then? And would anybody have even cared, except for how it might affect the pub's reputation?

The loneliness that she always felt deep in her heart surged outward, for a moment overwhelming everything. She pressed her bruised hands over her eyes, plunging herself into darkness, and forced herself to take another long, settling breath. Crying would not help. Panicking would not help.

But how much longer could she remain here, before something truly terrible happened to her that could not be undone?

CHAPTER FOURTEEN

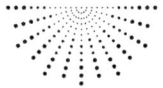

The following morning, Dora rose before dawn, as she always did. She pulled her sleeves down to cover her hands and hide the new bruises from sight, and then tied up her hair and hurried out to begin her day's work.

She did not encounter either her aunt or her uncle for several hours, but eventually, she heard them talking together in low voices in the kitchen. Normally, Dora would not dare to eavesdrop, but after the events of the previous night, she found herself lingering by the doorway, listening.

"I've had a few offers," Uncle Clifford was saying. "I told them we don't run that sort of establishment, but they're offering good money."

"It's time that girl started properly earning her keep," Aunt Maude replied. "We feed her and clothe her, and what income is she bringing in? She should be of use."

"Considering how I found her last night," Uncle Clifford said, "she's in no position to argue. The girl's already giving it away for free."

Aunt Maude made a noise of disgust. "After all we've given her," she said. "This is how she repays us? Risking the reputation of this place and not doing her job properly in the meantime?" She fell silent for a moment. "Did you see who it was, last night?"

"Gerald Cookson," Uncle Clifford said. "He's been coming by a lot more recently. Spending more too."

"Have a word with him, then," Aunt Maude said. "And anyone else we can trust that's approached you before. It won't take much effort on our part, I'm certain of that."

Dora crept slowly away, barely daring to breathe. Her heartbeat pounded in her ears, and she felt dizzy, like the floor was no longer level beneath her feet. That could not be her aunt and uncle's plan for her. They could not intend to commit such a sin. But she had heard them speak the words themselves. They had not known she was there. They probably would not have spoken if they had known. They planned to use her in the most shameful way, and once it began, she truly would have no escape. Where would she be able to go? Who would take her in, after that?

She needed to leave, immediately.

Dora crept back upstairs as quickly and quietly as she could. She had little in the way of possessions, but she could not leave with absolutely nothing. She gathered together what few things she felt she could truly call her own—her clothes, a coat and a solid pair of shoes—and shoved them into a bag. Was it worth sneaking out now, she wondered? Or should she wait until her aunt and uncle were asleep? If she waited, she risked giving her aunt and uncle time to spring their plan into action before she could escape. But if she acted now, in broad daylight, they might see her, and then any hope of escape would be lost.

She would have to wait. A few hours would not make a lot of difference. Once it was dark outside, and the pub was full of patrons, she would be more likely able to sneak out of the backdoor unseen. Of course, leaving at night had its own risks, including the simple fact that she had nowhere else to go, but it was no longer safe to remain here.

She briefly thought of her mama and papa, and their cottage together. She could hardly remember their faces now. They were merely blurs in her memory, full of warmth and affection, but marred by the truth she had long accepted, that she had not been good enough for them to love.

Could she go to them for help? Of course, she couldn't. She could not remember where they had lived, and that had been thirteen years ago. She carried their surname, but Wentworth was not particularly uncommon, and anything could have happened to them in the intervening years. Even if they were willing to offer her a little assistance, she would never be able to find them. They were the ones who would have needed to find her, and they had not, not for her years in the orphanage or her decade suffering under the rule of her aunt and uncle here.

No. Dora was on her own. She would have to find her own way.

She stashed her bag beneath the bed and returned to work.

Dora was tense the entire rest of the day. Every little creak of the floorboard made her jump, and every shout from her aunt or uncle sent terror coursing through her, even though each time they were only making mundane requests of her. Her hands shook whenever she let them rest, and as evening fell and the pub filled with customers, Dora could not stop herself from looking at each one in turn, wondering which might be part of her aunt and uncle's plan.

Finally, the customers departed as the hour grew late. Dora cleaned, as she always did, and then hesitated. Could she take a little money to help keep herself safe?

She had earned it, had she not, with all her years of work?

But she could not do it. Her conscience would not allow her to fall to the level of her so-called aunt and uncle. Another path would present itself, as long as she had faith. She wanted to leave this life behind, as cleanly as she could.

Dora climbed the staircase slowly, listening to the familiar creeks of the steps beneath her feet. Years spent walking up and down these stairs would prove vital tonight, as she needed her ascent to her room to be audible, and her descent and escape to be as silent as a whisper.

She slipped onto the attic landing and pushed open her bedroom door, clutching her lamp in her free hand. But there was already a lamp burning in her room, and a figure standing by the open window, looking out.

Dora gasped as Uncle Clifford turned to face her. Her bag of clothes lay torn open on the narrow bed beside him.

"Were you thinking of going somewhere, girl?" Uncle Clifford said in a low voice.

For a moment, Dora could not speak. It was as though all the air had been stolen from her lungs. Then she found herself shaking her head.

"You were planning on running away? Where would you go, Dora?"

Dora took a small step backwards. She glanced at the ruined bag. She *needed* those things. "I was just cleaning," she said. "I put the clothes away—"

"Don't lie to me!" Uncle Clifford shouted. Spittle flew from his lips, and Dora flinched. "Do not lie." He marched forward and grabbed Dora by the wrist. She hissed in pain as his hand clenched around the bruises left there by another man, less than a day before. "We take you in, we feed you, we clothe you, and *this* is what you do to your aunt and I? Do you have no respect?"

"*You* have no respect!" Dora cried, before she could stop herself. "I heard you talking. You were going to sell me to men for money. I can't—I won't—"

"You will do as we tell you!" Uncle Clifford shouted. "You will *thank us* for all we've done for you."

"If I'm so terrible," Dora said, "then why won't you let me go? Why would you want me here?"

He pulled on her wrist, hauling her closer. She stumbled into her bedroom. The attic space was so small that there was barely space for them both to stand inside. "We made an investment in you," he said. "I intend to profit from it."

Dora struggled, desperately trying to pull her wrist out of his grip, but he would not let go.

"You don't own me," she said. "I will not let you hurt me any more than you already have." She pulled harder, striking out with her other arm, and Uncle Clifford's grip on her arm slipped. She stumbled as she slid free, but Uncle Clifford was already reaching for her again, snatching at her hair. "No!" she shouted, as his fingers ripped into her scalp. "Let me go." She struggled against him, and he grabbed her neck.

"We own you," he repeated. "You need to learn some respect, girl." He shoved her backward, and she hit the window hard. Dora had a moment to register the shock and regret flashing on Uncle Clifford's face before momentum carried her backward, tumbling through the open window and down toward the street.

She was unconscious before she hit the ground.

CHAPTER FIFTEEN

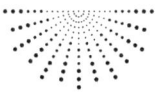

Clifford Brown did not see himself as an evil person. He worked hard, took good care of his wife, and had even fed and clothed an orphan for years when she would otherwise have had no one. He liked the gleam of money, but who in this world didn't? He could not stand insult or disrespect, but the fault then was not with him for reacting, but with his opponent for disrespecting him in the first place. He had protected the girl for years from the propositions of some of the inn's patrons, and she was the one who had thrown that all away. He had caught her red handed. She could not deny it! Was it wrong of him to see a profit when one presented itself? Wrong to expect that the girl would help repay the great debt she owed to his and his wife's kindness? No one of right mind would think so.

But when Clifford saw the girl tumble from the window with a shriek, he did, for a moment, feel regret. She landed with a dull thud, and Clifford stared at the window, breathing in and out, not daring to go and look at the state she was in. He had intended to frighten the girl, and maybe punish her for her rebelliousness, ensure that she did not leave. He certainly had not intended to send her falling out of the window.

"Clifford?" his wife cried. "What was that?"

Clifford turned and began quickly walking down the stairs. The girl could not be found below the window outside the inn. There would be questions if she was. It made sense, of course, that the girl might simply have fallen. Young women could be so thoughtless and clumsy, and her room was so high. But still, there would be questions, and questions led to the sort of attention that Clifford did not wish to endure. And if any passers-by had heard the girl's shouts before she fell, the accident would be much harder to explain.

He had not done wrong, of course. Her shouts had been irrational, the cries of a panicked, selfish child, but Clifford did not want to have to exert the effort required to prove that.

Luckily, the street outside the girl's room was deserted. The moon was thin that night, mostly hidden from view by the buildings around him, and the main lights of the inn had already been blown out, so Clifford found it difficult to see. But he could make out the crumpled shape of the girl. She was not moving.

"Girl," Clifford said. He leant down and pushed the shape. "Get up, girl." She still did not move. Her head lolled on her neck, and her limbs were limp. He could not tell if she was breathing. Either way, she could not be found here.

Clifford scooped the girl up in his arms and hurried away, muttering under his breath as he went. The main road to the docks was only a short walk away. No one would question the abandoned body of a girl there. A young woman might have come across any sort of trouble, none of which had any connection or relation to the inn several streets away.

The gas lamps illuminated the main street, but this road was thankfully deserted too. Clifford took the opportunity to look properly at the girl in his arms. The side of her dress was stained with blood, and red bubbled around her lips as well. If she was not already dead, she would be soon.

What a waste, he thought. Ten years, for it to come to this.

He placed her on the roadside, a little out of the lamplight, so that she would not be found until morning. And then he turned home, already thinking of how he might replace her.

Colette Green always liked to depart early for work. Her days were always hectic, rushing from patient to patient, with never enough time to give them all the care and attention that they deserved. She was run off her feet, providing comfort here, sewing up wounds there, even handing the instruments to the surgeon as he worked. Her days were filled with blood and sweat and not a little desperation, and although she loved her work, and loved the thought that she was making a difference in suffering people's lives, she always made sure she walked slowly to work, savouring a little time to breathe and think for herself.

Colette Green had been a young widow, and a childless one, and people had urged her to remarry within a year of her husband's death. He had been old, they insisted, and she was young. She had an entire life ahead of her. Colette agreed with them. She had done her duty by entering the state of marriage, and God had seen fit to release her from it at a young age. She intended to do as only widows could and be a woman who worked in the world without any other distractions and without any stain to her or her family's reputation.

She had served as a nurse in the Crimean war, sweating in the heat, sewing up the wounded and attending to the needs that the doctors felt too busy to notice—bathing the patients, changing their bandages, ensuring that things were as clean as it was possible for them to be. She barely slept in those days. Her skin itched under the constant bite of mosquitos, and there was always more work to be done, always another soldier who needed her help and could not wait until dawn.

The war ended, and Colette returned to England. While abroad, she might have thought that she would be glad to be free of the blood and the cries of suffering patients, if she had had any time to think at all, but as soon as she stepped onto English soil, she knew that her calling was not yet complete. Nurses were still a relatively new concept in England—too radical, some men said, too *German* an idea, and how could a woman really be trusted around blood? But Colette found a place that would value her contribution, and she had been working there now for over fifteen years.

It was a chilly autumn morning, but Colette still walked slowly, taking in the sight of the final stars in the sky. She greeted the milkman as he began loading his cart and smiled at the hazy light of the dying streetlamps.

Then she noticed a shape slumped against the wall at the side of the road. *Poor thing*, she thought immediately. Had they slept there all night? The lamplight illuminated a sliver of the person's face, along with dark hair. A woman. No, she realised, a girl, barely more than a child. What tragedy had brought her there?

Colette could certainly spare a penny for a poor homeless girl, but perhaps she should not wake her. Who knew what she had suffered before she fell asleep? Then Colette noticed the blood smeared down the girl's chin.

Colette ran to her and knelt in the dirt beside her. Now that she was closer, she could see that the girl was bleeding from her side, and one of her arms was bent at an unnatural angle. She had had an accident—maybe a fall—or someone had beaten her. Colette held her hand an inch in front of the girl's nose and mouth, and she sighed in relief when she felt the gentle movement of breath. Not dead then. At least, not yet. But she clearly needed help, and soon.

Colette was not a particularly large woman, but she picked up the skinny young girl with surprising ease. She was as light as a feather, Colette thought, in a way that suggested a lifetime of hunger.

The girl moaned softly as Colette took her first step toward the hospital, and Colette felt a spark of hope. If the girl was aware enough to respond, even in a slight manner such as that, then perhaps there was hope.

CHAPTER SIXTEEN

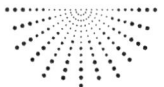

The first time Dora awoke, all she wanted to do was to fall asleep again. Her head pounded terribly, her arm felt strange and stiff, and she felt a strange pain in her stomach that seemed somehow woolly and far away. She could hear people talking around her, but she could not understand the words. Where was she? It did not feel like home. For a moment, she tried opening her eyes, but then the exhaustion overwhelmed her, and she fell unconscious again.

The next time Dora awoke, her head hurt less, but her stomach hurt more. Her throat was dry and sore, and she frowned for a moment, wondering where she was. Then she remembered. The argument with Uncle Clifford, her desperate attempt to escape from his grasp, the feeling of falling. Suddenly, she could not breathe. What had they done to her while she was unconscious?

She opened her eyes and sat up with a gasp, and then groaned as pain sparked in her stomach. She put a hand to her stomach and felt the bandages there.

"You're awake!"

An unfamiliar woman hurried towards her. She looked to be in her forties or maybe her early fifties, her face lightly wrinkled, her black hair salted with white. She was tall and sturdy looking, her hair pulled back into a tight twist, and she wore the black dress and large white apron of domestic help or a nurse.

"Who are you?" Dora asked. Her voice croaked, and her throat hurt to speak.

"My name is Colette," the woman said. "I'm a nurse here. You gave us quite a fright."

"How—" Dora looked around, taking in the rest of the room. She was lying in a long room filled with beds and sleeping patients that must be an infirmary. A couple of other woman, similarly dressed to Colette, tended to others.

Uncle Clifford could not have brought her here. He would be too afraid of the accusations and of the expense, and too little concerned with Dora's own safety. So how had she ended up here?

"I found you lying on the street," Colette said, "and brought you here. You were lucky. You looked like you had taken a large fall. You were in a bad way."

Dora's heart raced. "I don't have any money," she said quickly. How would she pay for this? Would she end up in debtors' prison, for expenses she had incurred while she was unconscious? Surely death would have been better than that.

"Now, don't fret," Colette said. "It isn't good for your recovery. You don't owe anybody anything. I found you, and the hospital owes me quite a bit, after all these years. Don't worry about that. But let me fetch the doctor. He can speak with you." She turned and took a few steps away, and then stopped and looked back. "What's your name, child?" she asked.

"Dora," Dora said. "Dora Wentworth."

"Do you have any family, Dora? Anyone who must be worried about you?"

Dora hesitated, and then she shook her head. Colette nodded sympathetically. "I'll just fetch the doctor, then," she said.

Dora lay back, trying to breathe. She had escaped, then. Hadn't she? She had needed to get away from Uncle Clifford and Aunt Maude, and here she was, injured but alive, out of their reach. Uncle Clifford must have thought her dying, if he had abandoned her by the side of the road. He would probably be too distracted with worry that her injuries might be traced back to him that he would not think to consider where she might have gone if she survived. Yet Dora could not feel the relief that should have come with such a realisation. Once again, she was alone in the world.

The doctor was a tall, greying man who seemed almost irritated by the need to speak with Dora. "You're lucky to be alive," he said to her, in a tone that suggested that she had been reckless, somehow. "Your arm was broken, and you had some internal bleeding, but little permanent damage was done."

"What do you mean?" Dora asked. *Little* did not mean *none*.

"You have sustained some internal bruising and scarring," the doctor said. "You are alive, but you will never have children."

Dora stared at him. His words rang inside her head, not seeming to make sense. "I cannot have children?" she repeated. Her throat ached.

"I am sorry," the doctor said, in the same unsympathetic tone as before. "But if you are to have any life after this at all, you need to rest. Do not allow yourself to become overly excited." He nodded, as though his work was all satisfactorily completed, and walked away.

Dora felt the hot burn of tears in her eyes as she lay back again. She could sense other people in the infirmary looking at her, obviously having overheard what the doctor had told her. She would not cry, she told herself. She would not cry. But the tears rolled down her cheeks unbidden, and the pain in her stomach swelled, making it difficult to breathe.

Not only was she alone, but she would always be alone. Ever since she was a young child, all Dora had wanted was a home and a family, a place that she could belong. And now that hope had been stolen from her. Uncle Clifford and Aunt Maude had stolen the possibility that she might be adopted by a family who would love her as a child, and now Uncle Clifford had stolen her hope of forging a family of her own. She would never have children. And could it be possible for any man to love her, if she could not give him the family he wanted? The sobs shuddered through her body, and she bit her lip to try and force them back, to prevent herself from making a sound.

She felt a gentle hand rest on her shoulder. When Dora opened her eyes, the nurse, Colette, was leaning over her, her face soft with sympathy. "There now, child," she said. "All will be well."

But Dora could not see how that could ever be true.

Dora remained in the infirmary for another week, with Colette watching over her. Perhaps it was because she had been the one to find the girl and bring her to the hospital, or perhaps it was just that the girl said she had no one, but Colette found she had a continuing desire to help her, above and beyond her usual care toward one of her patients. Physically, the girl was healing. Soon she would be well enough to leave the hospital, freeing up the bed for another patient who needed it more. But the girl seemed broken in spirit. She slept little and spoke even less, passing much of the time staring hopelessly at the ceiling or at the wall.

Colette worried what would become of the girl once she left the hospital. Dora had not revealed what had happened to bring about her injuries, but Colette had the strong suspicion that she had nowhere safe to return to. And how pointless it seemed for her to have saved the girl from death, only to abandon her to it again once her physical injuries were healed.

Colette longed to learn what had befallen the poor girl, but she knew that Dora was not yet ready to tell her, and she did not wish to pry or to increase her suffering.

Still, the girl needed a safe place to stay to continue her recovery. Colette was often busy with her work, and so would not make the best companion, but she was also an established widow with a career of her own, and that status brought certain privileges. She had a good house that she had been left by her husband, with ample space for another inhabitant. It was safe and warm, away from the docks and whatever had befallen the girl there. And over her years as a wife and then a widow, Colette had built a rather large, if eclectic, circle of acquaintances. Surely among them they could find a place for the girl to get back on her feet.

When Colette offered Dora a place to stay, Dora said very little. She wrapped her arms around herself, and thanked Colette in a quiet voice for her generosity. Her reaction only strengthened Colette's belief that she was doing the right thing. Dora needed help, and Colette was determined to provide it.

CHAPTER SEVENTEEN

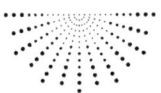

Dora had been saved by an angel. That was all that Dora could think when Colette Green welcomed her into her home. Barely two weeks before, Dora had been living under her aunt and uncle's rule, working tirelessly for no love and no pay, and on the verge of being forced into prostitution. She had expected that she would be homeless in order to escape.

Yet Colette had saved her. When Dora fell from that window, she should by all rights have died when she hit the ground. She had fallen three floors, onto the solid stone, with nothing to cushion her landing, and the only person who had witnessed the accident was a man who cared nothing for her survival. It was a miracle that Dora had survived the fall, a miracle that Uncle Clifford had abandoned Dora's limp body along Colette's path, a miracle that Dora had kept breathing until Colette found her in the pre-dawn light.

Colette could have ignored her. She could have brought her to the hospital and never thought about her again. Instead, she had welcomed Dora, an utter stranger, into her home, without any probing questions about her past or the accident that had brought her here. Dora did not have the words to express her gratitude. Colette Green had saved her life, but all Dora could do was whisper her thanks to her and hope that the depth of her emotion was clear in her eyes.

Colette Green lived in a neat two-story townhouse about a mile's walk from the docks. She had neither servants nor a cook—why bother, she told Dora, when she was the only person living here, and she was perfectly capable of caring for herself?—but she had a dining room separate from her kitchen, a study filled with old books, and two unoccupied bedrooms on the upper floor, one of which she now gave to Dora for her own use. It was the grandest house that Dora had ever been inside, and now it was to be her temporary home.

"My husband was quite well off, God rest his soul," Colette said over dinner on the night of Dora's arrival. "The study was his when he was alive. Well, the entire house was his, really, but the study in particular. It doesn't get much use now. Feel free to read anything you like."

"Oh," Dora said, and she felt herself blushing. She had learned her letters at the orphanage, before her aunt and uncle had taken her away, but they were little more than vague memories now. "I cannot read very well."

"There is no shame in that," Colette told her. "I only wish I had the time to teach you. I am at the hospital almost every hour I am awake."

"No, no, that's all right," Dora said. "You've done so much for me."

"It was the least I could do," Colette said. "And this house has always needed more life in it. It is too quiet with only me here."

Colette left early for the hospital the following morning, leaving Dora in the house alone. Dora immediately put herself to work, cleaning as much of the house as she could to try and earn her keep, but when Colette returned at the end of the day, she chided Dora for exerting herself when she was still recovering from her fall.

"You are my guest, Dora," she said. "You are supposed to be resting."

But resting was too quiet and still an activity for Dora. Whenever she thought about the accident, or remembered the doctor's blunt diagnosis, the sadness inside her threatened to overwhelm her, and she kept herself as busy as she could without entirely defying the nurse's orders.

Colette, for her part, continued to worry about her young guest. Although Dora was safe and fed, she continued to suffer from the demons that haunted her, and long days spent alone with little to do were not helping her the way company and activity would.

Although Colette was happy to help Dora, she also knew that Dora feared the thought of being a burden and would not truly settle and begin to heal until she believed herself useful.

Colette, therefore, gave Dora little tasks she could complete during her days, sending her on shopping errands to get her out in the fresh air, but she also began to reach out to her acquaintances to see if anyone might have a suitable situation for a polite young girl in need. Certainly, one of her friends must be looking for a maid or a nanny and could offer a home and an income in return for steady work. She also wrote to her nursing acquaintances in London, to see if Dora might find a place to learn there.

Colette was both surprised and relieved by the responses she received. While the nursing institute had no space for new students, and her acquaintances in Liverpool had no work available, she received a very gratifying letter from one Mr Calvin Adams, of York.

Colette had included Mr Adams in her efforts out of an abundance of optimism, and not because she truly expected him to respond. He had been a lively man once, but since the accident a year before, he had become something of a recluse. Colette could understand his manner, even if she did not think it did him any good. His wife had hurt him, both physically and in his heart, and he had come unthinkably close to losing his children. It would take time for those wounds to heal. He kept to himself now, and Colette had not seen him in over six months.

So, Colette was surprised to find a response from Mr Adams, and even more surprised when she opened it and read that he had a position that might be of interest to her young charge. Mr Adams was in need of a nanny to watch his young daughters, Ethel and Maeve, and had yet to find anyone he considered up to the task. If Mrs Green recommended her charge to the position, then Mr Adams would be willing to offer her the opportunity.

The question was how to broach the topic with Dora.

"You know, Dora," Colette said, as they ate dinner the following day, "that you are welcome here as long as you like. But I recently heard from one of my acquaintances, a good man named Calvin Adams in York. He has two darling daughters, aged three and five, I believe, and since his wife died in an accident last year, he has been caring for them alone. But the accident left him in fairly ill health as well, and he informs me he is looking for someone to help care for the little ones. I wondered if perhaps you might be interested."

Colette waited with baited breath as Dora considered her words. The position would be good for both Dora and Mr Adams, but it still depended on Dora seeing the merit in the plan. And although Dora had no friends or family in Liverpool, she might still be reluctant to leave the city she had called her home.

"York?" Dora asked cautiously.

"Yes," Colette said. "It's a wonderful medieval city in Yorkshire, about a hundred miles from here. It's smaller than Liverpool. More peaceful. And I've known Mr Adams for many years. He is a good man. A bit quiet these days; keeps to himself. But a good man, nonetheless. I think you might be happy there."

Dora nodded slowly. "I've never left Liverpool before," she said.

"I would go with you," Colette said. "I have a day away from work on Sunday. We could take the train there, and you could meet him. See if you find the situation suitable."

"The train," Dora repeated. She turned a little pale at the word.

Of course, Colette reminded herself. Dora was young and had seen little of the world. She had never ridden on the steam train or gone more than a few miles away from the place of her birth. A journey on those great inventions might be exciting, but it would be intimidating too.

Well, Colette thought. All the more reason for them to go. New experiences would be good for the girl after all that she had been through. She needed hope, and a promise that there was life beyond what she had suffered through thus far. And the endless energy of two young girls in her care would certainly keep both her hands and her mind busy as she continued to heal.

"We shall go," Colette said, with a decisive nod. "Even if you do not choose to accept the position, I would like a trip to York, and to see my friend again. You will love the old city walls, and the Minster, and the air is so much fresher there than it is here. And I know a wonderful teashop that we can indulge ourselves at."

Dora nodded. She began to pick at the skin around her fingernails. A nervous habit, Colette thought. "Is he—a kind man?" she asked slowly.

"Certainly," Colette said. "He will be a good employer, I'm certain of that. But we can see Sunday. And if you do not like anything about the situation, we can both travel back here the very next day. Yes?"

Dora nodded again, and Colette decided that would have to be agreement enough.

CHAPTER EIGHTEEN

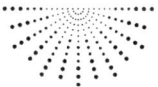

The metal beast waited at the end of the platform. Dora eyed it warily, taking in the chimneys that would soon be pouring out steam, and the soot-covered man currently standing by the driver's cart, talking to one of the station porters.

"This one is our carriage," Colette said, bustling past her. Some of the carriages had open sides and wooden benches crammed with people, but Colette led Dora to a blue carriage with a word that Dora could not read and a shiny gold *2* painted on the door. A porter moved to open the door for Colette, and Colette nodded her thanks as the pair of them climbed aboard.

"I think we might be lucky," Colette said, as she squeezed along the aisle and opened the door to a small compartment, with uncovered wooden seats on either side of the small window, facing one another. "We might get the compartment to ourselves." Colette sat down by the window, and Dora sat carefully opposite her.

"Have you travelled by train much before?" Dora asked her companion. She glanced warily out of the window as she spoke. The other platform was currently visible, but Dora knew that soon the train would be moving, and then she would see the countryside fly by, unnaturally fast. She gripped the base of her seat and tore her eyes away.

"Oh, yes," Colette said. "I've travelled quite far as a nurse. In the old days, you know, third class was all open, without a roof and no seats, like a cattle car. You would get jolted about constantly by the train, so much that sometimes it was difficult not to fall over. The number of strange gentlemen I seized by the arm to keep myself steady!" She laughed. "It is all more civilised now."

Dora nodded, then fought back a yelp of surprise, as the train whistle tore through the air, and the carriage began to move.

"Do not worry," Colette said. "It's all perfectly safe."

Dora did not see how that could be true. The train made a terrible noise, like the roaring of a beast, and the view from the window was soon obscured by a trailing blanket of black smoke. The wheels clattered beneath them, rattling almost too loud for her to hear Colette's words, and Dora felt herself being jolted side to side by the rhythm of the train.

Still, Dora did not complain, and once she became accustomed to the noise and the movement, she allowed herself to admit that perhaps there was something exciting about travelling on this grand new technology. When the train pulled into a station and Colette stood, Dora let out a sigh of relief, glad the ordeal was over, but after disembarking, Colette simply led them to another train that was travelling on a different line, and the whole thing started over again. They transferred trains one more time on their journey, but finally, they pulled into a grand station with an arched ceiling high, high above them, and Colette smiled.

"Here we are," she said. "York."

Colette led Dora up the stairs and across a bridge that stood above the many lines. Dora paused halfway across and rested her hands on the wooden railing, looking down at the trains and the people below her.

"This way, Dora!" Colette said, and Dora hurried after her again, toward a large clock at the end of the bridge and stairs leading down toward the main concourse. Everything gleamed with modernity, and Dora had to force herself to keep pace with her chaperone, turning her head every which way and taking in every sight she could as she went.

The road outside the station was full of horses and carriages, and cab drivers shouted at Dora and Colette as they passed, asking them where they wished to go. Colette ignored them.

"It isn't far," she said. "We can walk." She glanced up at another clock, hanging from the metal veranda outside the station. "We should go directly to Mr Adams's. He will be expecting us."

They walked along the road, following the curve of a crumbling wall that looked as though it had stood there since the time of the terrifying Vikings, if not before. In the distance, atop the hill, Dora saw a grand cathedral, its stone towers and multi-coloured windows gleaming in the midday sun. They crossed a large river, its water high against the paths that ran alongside it, and the ruined remains of what Colette informed her had once been a monastery, before Colette led her off the main road onto a side street. The large cathedral was before them now, the city walls standing at their backs, as Colette approached a white-walled house with an iron gate.

Colette tried to open the gate, but it was locked.

"Mr Adams!" Colette cried. "Mr Adams, are you here?"

"I'm coming!" a gruff voice shouted from the house. Dora could feel her hands shaking at the prospect of meeting her new employer, so she clutched them tightly in front of her, hoping she looked suitably demure.

But the man who emerged from the house was dressed in the uniform of a butler. He was grey and grizzled, his back bent over almost double, but he walked with a confident step across the yard and toward the gates.

"Mrs Green?" he said, as he drew level with them. "And Miss Wentworth?"

"The very same," Colette said.

The butler nodded. "The master has been expecting you."

Dora could feel her heart pounding against her chest. Exactly how rich *was* Mr Adams? She had known he must have some money, to be able to pay for help to care for his children, but Dora had imagined him like Colette. Rich by all the standards that Dora had ever known, with a sizeable house and money to spare, but not a walled off enclave with a little land of his own, even in the middle of a city. Not a house rich enough to employ a butler. Dora did not know much about rich houses, but she imagined that if a man could employ someone to answer the door and polish the silver, then they must have multiple maids and a cook as well. How could Dora possibly fit in here?

The butler unlocked the gate and bowed as Colette and Dora walked inside. He closed the gate after them and locked it immediately, and the clank of the metal rang in Dora's ears as the butler led them toward the house.

"This is Mr Finch," Colette said to Dora. "He has worked with Mr Adams for, oh— thirty years now?"

"I have been with the Adams family for over forty years, ma'am," Mr Finch said. "Since before Mr Adams was born."

"Ah, yes, I remember now," Colette said. "Arthur was good friends with Mr Adams's father," she added to Dora. "I met Mr Adams himself when he was as small as his young children are now. It is difficult to think, sometimes, that so many years have passed. And are you well, Mr Finch?"

"Very well, ma'am," Mr Finch said.

"And the girls?"

"I am certain that the master could tell you far better than I, ma'am," Mr Finch said. "But they are a lively pair."

Mr Finch led them into the house's grand entrance hall, and Dora had to exert all of her self-control to prevent herself from staring at everything they passed. The walls were covered in deep red paper, with golden-coloured brackets on the walls to hold the gas lamps. The wooden floor beneath their feet was polished so much that it gleamed, and all of their footsteps echoed as Mr Finch led them down the hall.

"The master is in his study," he wheezed. He paused outside a heavy wooden door and knocked. "Sir," he said. "Mrs Green and Miss Wentworth to see you."

"Show them in, Finch," the man said. Mr Finch opened the door and ushered Dora and Colette inside.

Dora found herself stepping into a large study. Two of the walls were covered floor to ceiling with books, while the third contained sizeable windows that let in plenty of light. An imposing oak desk took up most of the space in the middle of the room, so large that for a moment it distracted her from the man sitting behind it.

Calvin Adams did not rise when the two women entered his study, opting instead for a respectful nod. Dora was in no position to judge a man of his wealth, but she found it immediately odd. She had thought the upper class were very fond of the rituals of good manners. Even if Mr Adams did not think Dora worthy of such respect, he must surely owe it to his long-time friend, Colette.

Based on what Colette had told her, Dora knew that Mr Adams must be in his early thirties, but her first impression was of a man much older than that. His thick dark hair was streaked with grey, and frown lines ran down his forehead. The dark circles under his eyes suggested a man who did not get adequate sleep, while his strong nose and well-defined chin gave the impression of someone stubborn, possibly even sullen. He wore fine clothes, but they were slightly worn. It could not be that he could not afford to replace them, Dora thought, as he clearly had ample resources at his disposal. Instead, she got the sense that he was a man who simply had not cared to do so, unconcerned by his appearance.

"My dear Mr Adams!" Colette said. "It has been too long since we have seen one another."

"Yes, Mrs Green," Mr Adams said. He gave her a brief smile, and then his face fell into a frown again. "Yes, it has been some time." He spoke heavily, as though the past were something he did not wish to recall. "But I was glad to hear from you. And I am glad to see you well."

"Calvin," Colette said, with a conspiratorial little smile, "allow me to introduce Miss Dora Wentworth, a recent ward of mine. Miss Wentworth, this is Mr Calvin Adams, a long-time friend of mine."

Dora bobbed into a curtsey, uncertain if she was expected to speak.

"Yes, yes," Mr Adams said, in a tone that suggested he wished to conclude the conversation as quickly as possible. "You suggested her as a nanny for my girls. Do you have any experience taking care of children, Miss Wentworth?"

Dora glanced uncertainly at Colette. "No, sir," she said. "But I am a hard worker. I would not let you down."

"Well," Mr Adams said, "that remains to be seen. Still, it would be difficult for you to be worse than the last girl."

Dora did not know what the proper thing to say in response to that could possibly be, so she said nothing. But Colette gave Mr Adams an affectionate scowl.

"You are too harsh, Calvin," she said. "You always have been, ever since you were a child. I promise you, Miss Wentworth comes with my full recommendation."

"Yes," Mr Adams said. "That is why I invited you. Well, I suppose you had best meet the girls before any decision is made. I believe they're in the playroom with Nancy, one of the maids. I am afraid I cannot accompany you," Mr Adams added, "but I am deep in my work. Finch will show you the way."

"You are not getting out of things so easily," Colette said. "I insist on us having tea before I return to Liverpool."

"By all means," Mr Adams said with a thin smile. "I am merely a little distracted at present."

"Very well," Colette said. "Come along, Dora." Colette bustled out of the study and started for the stairs without waiting for Mr Finch's guidance. Dora hurried along beside her, wondering if she should speak. Mr Adams was not what she had expected a friend of Colette's to be. He seemed cold and detached, even with his lifelong friend, and manners seemed lost on him. Dora could not imagine that Colette would care for someone who was cold hearted or cruel, so she was not afraid of the strange man in the study, but there was certainly something rather severe about him that unsettled her.

"Please, Mrs Green," Mr Finch said, as he clamboured after her. "Allow me to show you the way."

Mr Finch led them up two flights of stairs and into a large, sunlit room. The playroom was in chaos. Dolls' clothes were strewn across the floor, while several dollies lay naked in a pile on one side. Drawing pencils had been broken underfoot, and half-finished pieces of artwork were crumpled and scattered about.

The room also contained a large dollhouse and a half-emptied chest of toys. There were also a couple of school desks in one corner, but they were the only things in the room that looked pristine.

A very tired-looking young woman sat in a rocking chair in another corner, her eyes fixed on the mending work in her hands. A small girl with wild brown ringlets lay on her stomach on the floor beside her, her legs swinging in the air, drawing on a scrap of paper. She did not look up as the strangers entered the room.

At first, Dora could not see the other girl that might be her charge. Then she spotted a small figure half-engulfed in a wardrobe, elaborate clothes and costumes piled around her. A large old-fashioned hat, decorated with an entire stuffed bird, fell down over her eyes, and her arms were covered with frayed silk gloves that extended all the way up to her armpits. She spun around at the sound of the newcomers and met Dora and Colette with an imperious gaze.

"Who are you?" she asked.

"Now, Miss Adams," Mr Finch said. "That's no way to greet guests."

"So you're guests?" the girl asked. "Have you come for tea?"

Dora imagined there must be a child's tea set somewhere in this playroom, but she had no idea how the girl would ever be able to locate it in all the chaos. The room contained more treasures than Dora had owned in her entire lifetime, abandoned and tossed aside like they meant nothing. Dora had spent many nights shivering beneath a thin blanket, and long winter days wrapped in shawl inadequate against the cold, and these girls had an entire wardrobe full of old clothes that might have warmed an entire orphanage, just for their games. It was difficult for Dora to believe. Could she really care for children who lived such a spoiled existence?

"This is Miss Wentworth and Mrs Green," Mr Finch said to the girl. "Miss Wentworth here might be joining us in the house soon."

That made the woman in the corner look up. "You're the new nanny?" she asked. Before Dora could answer either way, the woman barrelled on. "Oh, thank Heavens. We're in desperate need. The last one had no mettle to her. She barely lasted two weeks."

"Two weeks?" Dora repeated. "Why did she leave?"

"Miss Wentworth," Mr Finch said, before the woman could reply. "May I introduce you to Ethel," he gestured at the older girl scribbling on the floor, "and Maeve."

"I'm three!" Maeve said helpfully. "How old are you?"

"Sixteen," Dora said.

Maeve frowned. "That's old."

"Well," Dora said, "it's older than you."

Maeve shook her head. "It's just old." She turned back to the wardrobe. "Would you like to wear one of my hats?"

"I'm all right, thank you," Dora said.

"You speak funny," Maeve said, as she dug inside the wardrobe again.

"I'm not from here," Dora said. "I'm from Liverpool."

"Is that far?" asked Ethel from her place on the floor.

"It's about a hundred miles," Colette said. "We just came here this morning on the steam train."

"The steam train?" Ethel scrambled to her feet. "I went on the steam train once, with mamma. Papa doesn't allow us out now, though. Not even in the carriage. He sold the horses, even my Diamond."

"You had your own horse?" Dora asked her.

"A pony," Ethel corrected. "Mamma said she was going to teach me how to ride. But papa sold her."

"I'm certain he had a good reason," Dora said.

Ethel frowned but did not argue.

"Well," the maid said, as she stood. "If you're taking over, I'll be off, then."

"Oh, I—I haven't accepted the position yet," Dora said. The maid stared at her.

"Well, you better," she said. "We need the help. As long as you're not planning to just walk off, like the last one. I'm not a nanny, you know. It's not my job to be here."

Could Dora possibly join this household? She knew she could not afford to be choosy, even though Colette would certainly take her back to Liverpool if she asked. Yet what would life be like here? The children seemed spoiled and unruly, their father cold and uncaring. The house had a great air of oppression about it, like everyone was afraid to breathe too loudly.

"Why don't we take a walk, Dora?" Colette asked. "Take in some more of the city."

Dora nodded gratefully, and they left the chaotic playroom. The maid glared after them as they departed.

CHAPTER NINETEEN

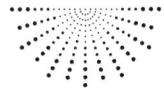

"I realise he is an unusual man," Colette said, as she and Dora walked down the cobblestone street together. "He has been through much hardship. But I can assure you that he has a good heart beneath it all."

Dora nodded. She trusted Colette's judgement, yet a *good heart* was not what she had seen. He seemed to have a distracted heart, at best, if not an uncaring one. And the children....

"The girls seem lonely," Dora said.

"I am certain that they are," Colette said sadly. "Life has not been easy for them."

"May I ask—what happened to their mother?"

Colette was silent for a long moment, considering. "She left them," she said eventually. "Several months ago. Things have been difficult for them all since then."

Now Dora saw how things were. The girls' mother had abandoned the family. Perhaps, Dora thought, she had run away with another man. Their father was left to deal with the aftermath, but he did not wish to see children who reminded him of his wife and her infidelity. The mother had sinned, and the daughters were being punished for it. Instead of having both parents, they now had no one.

It made Dora's heart ache. She understood what it meant to have your parents abandon you or push you away. She knew what it was like to grow up without love, where the best feeling you could hope for from your caregivers was one of weary obligation, and where even that was not guaranteed. The girls were acting bold and foolish because they had no one to guide them. They had no love left in their lives, except what they could offer each other, and based on how little they had interacted while Dora was in the room, even that seemed to be a struggle at present.

They were surrounded by people and possessions. They would never go hungry, or truly feel the cold, and they had more toys than Dora could ever have dreamed of. But they were lonely. They were deprived of love. And truly, Dora thought, was that not the most harmful deprivation of all?

"I think," Dora said slowly, "I should like to stay."

"You'll accept the job?" Colette asked with a smile.

Dora nodded. "I want to help the girls," she said.

"You will," Colette said. "And your presence will be good for Mr Adams too, you mark my words."

Dora had little interest in being good for Mr Adams, unless it meant encouraging him to soften toward his daughters again. But she nodded anyway.

"Well," Colette continued, "when we return, we can discuss the terms. I'm certain the housekeeper, Mrs Leigh, will be able to help us there. I am so pleased you have decided to remain here, Dora. I really believe you will do good here. And I suspect the girls will be good for you as well."

Dora had not even considered the concept of payment when accepting the position. She was too used to working for room and board, and to dismissing the value of her own work. So when Mrs Leigh offered her twenty pounds a year as salary, along with a room next to the girls' and meals with the other servants, Dora found herself momentarily speechless. Twenty pounds was more money than she could imagine. If she worked hard, and saved her income, it would only take a few years before she had the savings to support herself and take her wherever she wished. And if her new master turned out to be cruel, or some other emergency arose, her weekly salary guaranteed that she would not be trapped and helpless, as she had been before.

Dora wanted to throw her arms around Mrs Leigh in joy when the salary was agreed, but she succeeded in restraining herself. Dora had no possessions of her own, beyond the clothes that Colette had given her, so there would be no difficulty in moving in. Dora could start work immediately, and after several weeks of pain and idleness, she was relieved to do so.

Unfortunately for the maid in the playroom, however, an immediate start did not mean immediately caring for the girls. Mrs Leigh had many rules and instructions to impart to Dora, and she wanted to ensure that Dora understood every single one before taking up her position.

"You should write these down," Mrs Leigh said briskly. "I won't have you forgetting, and I can't always be here to answer your questions at all hours of the day when things come up."

Dora felt herself blushing. "I can't read or write, Mrs Leigh," she said. "I know a few letters…"

"You can't *read?*" Mrs Leigh repeated. Dora could see the shock on her face. "Well, I suppose you are only a nanny, not a governess. We did *have* a governess for about a month, but she took another position elsewhere. I cannot imagine why." Her tone suggested that, in fact, she knew precisely the reason. "At least we have found *somebody*. We can concern ourselves with their education later." She sighed. "Well, then. Listen closely. I do not want to repeat this."

The rules were numerous, but Dora had a sharp mind, and she was accustomed to memorising long lists of ever-changing demands from her aunt and uncle, so she did not think they would be too difficult to remember. The girls were to rise at 6 a.m., which meant that she must rise at 5:30 and be prepared to wake them and get them ready for the day. The girls were not allowed in any of the downstairs rooms without permission, particularly the master's study, and Dora was to ensure that they did not disturb the master's work with noisy play or any demands on his time. Mealtimes were strict, their diets already decided by the cook, and Dora was to eat with them.

The strangest rule, at least to Dora's mind, was that she was forbidden to take the girls in a carriage ride for any purpose. "If you wish to take them on an outing," Mrs Leigh said, "then you must clear it with the master first, and you must only travel by foot. If the master hears that the girls have stepped out without his permission, you will lose your job, and I will probably lose mine too. He doesn't keep a carriage here himself anymore, of course, but there are to be no cabs, no rides with friends, and absolutely nothing to do with the omnibus."

"Do the girls have a fear of carriages, ma'am?" Dora did not consider a carriage to be an essential part of life—she had certainly never ridden in one—but it seemed odd to her that such a convenience would be expressly and permanently forbidden when a person could easily afford it.

"The master does not like them," Mrs Leigh said, in a tone that would brook no argument or further questions. "We must follow his wishes in all things."

"Yes, ma'am," Dora said. She thought again of that strange, cold, blunt man she had met in the study, and the wild girls she had seen, almost entirely ignored in their playroom. It seemed that Mr Green's only interest in the children was in setting rules for them, and she felt another wave of pity for them. She knew what it was like to be neglected by the people who were supposed to love and care for you.

She was given a room in the attic, next to the girls' playroom, and Dora had to school her face to hide her amazement at how spacious and comfortable it looked. Clean sheets covered the bed, and a neat uniform hung in the wardrobe. The window was small, which she was thankful for, but it let in light and air, and Dora thought that she could be happy here. It would certainly suit her better than being in Colette's grand, empty house alone, desperately wishing to be useful.

Dora bid Colette a tearful goodbye, and the two women embraced. "Oh, don't cry, now," Colette said, patting Dora on the arm. "We will see each other again. I have the perfect reason to visit York more often, now, do I not?"

"I will try and learn to read," Dora said, "so that I can read any letters you might send me, even if I cannot write back."

"Then I will send you plenty of letters to practice with," Colette said. "But I insist that you write back as well. I won't mind what you say, but you can't learn if you don't practice forming the words yourself too, now, can you?"

Dora promised Colette that she would try, and Colette departed, leaving Dora in this strange new city alone.

CHAPTER TWENTY

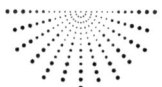

Despite the strictness of the rules given to Dora by Mrs Leigh, it was clear that the girls had not faced any real discipline in some time. Dora rose before dawn on her first morning on the job and dressed in her neat uniform, but when she went to wake the two girls, Maeve protested loudly, and Ethel just pulled her blankets up over her head, as though that might make Dora forget she was there. Dora did not want to start their relationship off on the wrong foot or shout at the girls on her very first day, but she worried what would happen if she was unable to get the girls to follow the rules, and she also thought that perhaps the children needed a little more strictness and discipline in their lives.

Dora had been the same age as these girls when she lived at the orphanage, where strict rules were expected but nobody actually watched the children all that carefully to see if they were being followed. Dora had learned there that a lack of enforced rules and expectations was its own sort of neglect, likely to inspire a great loneliness in the girls. So, Dora persisted, and eventually managed to coax the girls into their day clothes and down for breakfast.

"Why did you come here instead of staying in Liverpool?" Maeve asked her, as she spooned porridge into her mouth.

"Don't talk with your mouth full," Dora said.

"Why not?" Maeve asked.

"Because it's *rude*," Ethel said. "Mamma said we had to act like real ladies."

"Well, I'm not a lady," Maeve said. "I'm a girl. Why did you leave Liverpool? Don't you miss your family?"

"I don't have a family," Dora said softly. "Liverpool was not a kind place to me. I think York will be better."

"York is better," Ethel said in a decisive voice. "We have Mr Nickols's sweet shop on the corner, but we're not allowed to go there anymore."

"Lemon drops!" Maeve shouted. "Do you like lemon drops?"

"I've never had any," Dora admitted. Maeve gaped at her.

"But you're so old," she said. "How have you not had lemon drops?"

"I don't know," Dora said. "I've never had the chance."

"Can we get lemon drops today! We can go to Mr Nickols's! Can we?"

"Your father wants you to stay here, I think."

Maeve groaned dramatically, wriggling on her chair. "We *always* stay here. We used to go out! And you're our nanny. You can say we can go, can't you?"

Dora considered the two girls before her. They were so full of energy, and seemingly desperate for attention. A walk outside would certainly do them some good. But it seemed a lot for her to request on her first day….

But she was in charge of their wellbeing now, wasn't she? And she had been told that all outings had to be approved by Mr Adams, not that no outings could be approved at all. "If you're good," Dora said, "I'll ask your father later and see what he says. But only if you're good."

Maeve bounced in her chair in excitement, but Ethel stared at her empty bowl and sighed. "He'll say no," she said.

"Then he says no," Dora said. "You have to respect your father, and trust he knows what is best for you." But as Dora said it, she found herself hating the words. People had said similar things about her aunt and uncle to her when she was younger. If she had continued to believe them, she would still be trapped there now, suffering the worst abuses at their hands, if she was even still alive at all. "I'll ask him," she said.

The playroom was still in the same state of chaos that it had been in the previous day, and Dora considered it all for a moment, hands on her hips, while Ethel ran to grab her alphabet book and Dora dashed to her dressing-up cupboard. "First things first," she said. "We have to make everything tidy, so your father will be impressed with you."

"Papa never comes here anymore," Ethel said. She was already staring at the first page of her book.

"Never, never, never," Maeve sang.

"He used to?" Dora asked.

"Before mama left," Ethel said. "Sometimes. I don't think he loves us any more now."

"Now I know that cannot be true," Dora said, but Ethel shook her head.

"It is," she said. "It's because of what mama did. He thinks it's our fault."

Maeve paused by the open cupboard. "I miss mama," she said, in a very quiet voice.

"Well you can't," Ethel said, matter-of-factly. "She's gone and she's not coming back. Not ever."

Maeve burst into noisy tears, and Dora ran across the room to put a comforting arm around her. "There, there," she said. "There now. It's all right."

"I miss—ma—mama," Maeve sobbed.

"I know," Dora said. She did not dare ask what had happened to their mother. She had heard from Colette that there had been an accident, but she did not know the details, and she did not wish to hurt the children more by forcing them to recollect it. "Come along," she said, in as cheerful a voice as she could muster. "Let's clean up the playroom, and then we can go out to Mr Nichols's and get some sweets. Yes?"

"Lemon drops?" Maeve asked, wiping her eyes with the back of her hand.

"And more," Dora said. "And we can even pass by the park on our way home if you like."

This was more than enticement enough for Maeve. She immediately spun around and scampered to the nearest pile of clothes, scooping them up in her arms.

It was barely seven in the morning, and Dora was already exhausted. The children were bold and strong willed, with a lot of pain in their hearts, but Dora found that she liked them, unruliness and all. She could tell that they were truly sweet girls, and they needed help that no one else was offering them.

And the exhaustion was exhilarating, in a strange way. Dora had been weighed down by her sadness since the accident; and even before then, she had always felt panicked and unsafe and desperately alone. The girls were keeping her so busy that she had no time to think of sadness, and how could anyone feel lonely with two children such as these?

The morning passed quickly, and the girls soon began to pester Dora about their promised outing. Dora was nervous about addressing Mr Adams on her first day, but a promise was a promise, and, she thought, the girls truly would benefit from the fresh air and change of scenery. Her duty now was to them and to their wellbeing, and she could manage a few nerves and a little discomfort if it would help them.

Just before noon, Dora walked down the main staircase and approached the study where she had met Mr Adams the day before. The door was slightly ajar.

Dora knocked lightly on the door. A long pause followed, and Dora was considering knocking again when she heard Mr Adams call, "Enter."

Dora pushed the door open. It creaked on its hinges as she stepped over the threshold and into the study.

The room was dimly lit, the heavy curtains pulled tight across the windows, blocking out the sun. A fierce fire roared in the fireplace, despite the relative warmth of the day, and the only other illumination was a lamp atop Mr Adams's desk.

Mr Adams himself sat close to the fire. He did not look up from the papers in front of him as Dora entered. She waited for him to acknowledge her, feeling it would be rude and presumptuous to address him first, but when he spoke, he was plainly irritated by the delay. "Yes?" he asked, still not looking up.

"I wanted to ask your permission to take the girls on an outing this afternoon, sir," she said. "I think the fresh air will do them good, and they are very excited to—"

"No," Mr Adams said. He turned over the sheet of paper he was reading, still not looking at her.

"But I haven't told you where I wish to take them yet," Dora said, stunned.

"It is irrelevant," Mr Adams said. "The girls are not to leave the house."

"But sir," Dora said quietly. "The girls need—"

"You made your request," Mr Adams said. "I refused it. Is there anything more?"

Dora gaped at him, lost for words. How could he be so cold and uncaring?

"Then go," Mr Adams said, when she did not speak. "I have work to do."

And Dora obeyed.

CHAPTER TWENTY-ONE

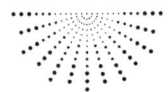

Maeve cried heartily when Dora told her of her father's judgement, but Ethel remained silent, a serious expression on her face. The older sibling did not even really appear disappointed, merely resigned. She had known all along what her father's answer would be, and she had never let hope truly bloom in her heart.

Dora got a lecture from Mrs Leigh that evening when she descended to the kitchen for her supper.

"To think that you bothered the master with so frivolous a thing! It reflects badly on all of us."

"I'm sorry, ma'am," Dora said. She wanted to argue that Mrs Leigh had told her that she needed to seek Mr Adams's permission before taking the girls out of the house, but she knew that such an argument was both impertinent and useless. She now realised that asking permission was a façade, that he would never approve the girls' departure, because he did not truly care for their wellbeing at all. Dora's heart broke for the girls, but she could not regret trying on their behalf.

The days passed, and Dora's sympathy for Ethel and Maeve grew into real, deep affection. They were clever, creative children with strong opinions and even stronger wills, and although Dora could not have said that working with them was easy, every day was as fulfilling as it was exhausting. Slowly, piece by piece, these two young girls began to mend Dora's heart, and she became dedicated to helping them, however she could.

Eventually, Dora's first Sunday off arrived. Dora woke at her usual time out of habit, and found herself looking around her room, wondering what she should do with herself. She had never had free days at her aunt and uncle's.

She eventually decided to go out and explore the city, and she had a thrilling morning walking through the winding streets, looking at the bookbinders and the tailors, going to see the castle tower and the ancient city walls. For the first time in her life, she had some money of her own, and she purchased a little lunch from a stall at the market and handed out much of the rest to beggars and flower sellers that she passed.

Finally, as she wandered her way back home, she saw a tall, narrow building on the street corner, with the sign *Mr Nichols's Spectacular Sweets* above the door. Dora hurried over and pushed open the swinging door. A bell rang above her head as she stepped inside and took in the sights and sounds of the shop.

A group of children were clamouring at the counter, behind which a stooped and somewhat wizened older man stood, weighing boiled sweets on his scales. The shelves on the wall behind his head were crammed full of large glass jars, and each jar was stuffed with a different, brightly coloured sweet. Handwritten labels on the jars explained their contents, but Dora could not read them. Instead, she marvelled at the swirling pink and yellow of one sweet, and the deep black of another. There were a couple of yellow options. One of them must be Maeve's beloved lemon drops.

Dora waited behind the children to approach the counter. When her turn came, the man gave her a wide, mostly toothless grin. "Ah, good afternoon, miss. What can I do for you today?"

"I would like a bag of lemon drops," Dora said. She pulled a couple of her remaining pennies from her pocket and held them out to him.

"Well, now, this will buy you quite an amount," the man said. "I haven't seen you before. Are you visiting the city, miss?"

"I recently moved here," Dora said. "I am working for Mr Adams as a nanny for his children, Ethel and Maeve."

"Ethel and Maeve," the man said, with a sigh. "How are the girls? I've missed seeing them. Maeve must have grown a lot since I saw her last."

"They are well," Dora said. "Although…" She hesitated. If she told the proprietor that the girls were not allowed to leave the house, it might sound like a criticism of her employer. And although she did want to criticise him, very much, that did not seem like a wise course of action. "I am buying these sweets for them. Maeve told me that lemon drops are her favourite."

"Well, send them my regards," the man said. He turned to the shelf behind him and picked up a large jar full of round yellow sweets. He placed it on the counter beside him, and then picked up a metal scoop and began to transfer the sweets onto his weighing scales. "It's a tragedy, what happened to them. Losing their mother like that."

Dora knew she should not gossip, so she did not reply, but she burned with curiosity.

"Well, it was foolish of their mother to run away like that," the man said. "She deserved what happened to her. But to harm the girls and Mr Adams in that way? It is the blessing of God that both girls survived. But of course, I have not seen them since."

"Not even once?" Dora asked.

"Oh, no," the man said. "Not at all. Mr Adams is too afraid of losing them to let them wander too far from him now. It is not surprising, after what occurred with his wife. But it is sad for them all."

It took all of Dora's self-control to fight the urge to ask more about what had occurred. It was not her business, she told herself, as she paid for the bag of lemon drops and wished the man good day. It would not be proper to ask. But she did yearn to know.

When Dora returned to the manor, she went in search of the girls. As it was her day off, she did not need to see them the entire day if she did not wish to, but after only a few hours, Dora missed the two girls. They had quickly become such an important part of her life that their absence seemed wrong.

She heard them before she saw them. Maeve was screaming and crying in the playroom, drowning out Dora's replacement's attempts to soothe her.

"I want Dora!" Maeve sobbed. "Where is Dora?"

"Hush, now, Maeve," Dora said, as she stepped into the room. "I do hope you're not misbehaving for Miss Beth."

The young maid, Miss Beth, knelt beside the screaming Maeve, her face white with panic.

"She won't stop crying," Miss Beth said.

Maeve looked at Dora and sniffed loudly. "Where did you go?" she said.

"Where did I go?" Dora repeated. She sat down on the floor next to Maeve. "I went into the city. But you had Miss Beth to look after you."

Maeve shook her head vehemently. "Want *you* here," she said.

"Well, I can't be here every hour of every day," Dora said. "Sometimes I have to go do other things. But I'll always come back."

Maeve hiccupped. "I thought—I thought you'd left us."

"Left you?" Dora said. Her heart sank. "Why would you think that?"

"You—you didn't come."

"I told you Miss Beth would be caring for you to today."

Maeve just continued to cry.

"Hush now, hush," Dora said. "I haven't left you. I am here, aren't I? And I don't plan to leave you. I even brought us all a little treat from my outing, but you can only have it if you're good. You are good, aren't you, Maeve?"

Maeve sniffed and nodded. "What sort of treat?" she asked, as she rubbed the tears from her eyes.

Dora pulled out the paper bag full of sweets. "Mr Nichols sends his regards."

"Lemon drops!" Maeve stopped crying at once. She bounced up and down on the spot in excitement as Dora called Ethel over. Miss Beth slipped out of the room, looking highly relieved, and Dora, Maeve and Ethel all settled in the middle of the playroom floor to share Dora's bounty.

When Dora first placed a lemon drop in her mouth, she was surprised by how sweet it was. She sucked on it slowly, wanting to make it last as long as possible. Ethel did the same, while Maeve crunched hers as soon as she was able.

"I wish we could see Mr Nichols," Ethel said softly, after a while.

"You will soon," Dora said. "Your father is just worried about you. He wants to keep you safe."

"From the sweetshop?" Ethel asked, sounding unconvinced.

"From everything," Dora said. She did not know much about what had happened with his wife, but she said what she could. "He was very worried for you after the accident. He is scared of losing you."

"Then why don't we ever see him?" Ethel said softly.

"He's a very busy man," Dora said. "But he loves you both very much." The words felt like a lie. How could he love the girls, and treat them as he did? Dora had very little experience, but she was certain that people did not hurt those they loved.

Ethel seemed equally unconvinced by Dora's words, and Dora's heart broke for the girls once more.

CHAPTER TWENTY-TWO

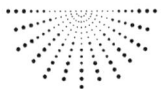

Despite all of Dora's doubt, Calvin Adams did love his two daughters very much. But that love was infected by fear, and that made him cold and distant. Calvin had come unbearably close to losing his daughters once before, at the hands of a woman he had trusted beyond anyone. How could he risk the thought of losing them again?

Seeing the girls reminded him of his past lost, his past failings, and of how much he still had to lose, and so he spent little time with them, preferring to retire to his study and keep his mind busy with work. His leg hurt constantly, an ever-present reminder of tragedy and betrayal, so he remained close to the roaring fire, hoping that the heat might soothe it. Sometimes the effort worked; sometimes it did not.

On the rare occasions that Calvin allowed his thoughts to wander, he inevitably returned to the question of whether he had done the right thing. Perhaps, he thought, he should have let his wife Lois and his daughters go. Then the girls would still have their mother, and he would not be in such physical pain. The emotional pain, he thought, would be more bearable than the combination he suffered now.

Lois had absconded with their daughters and her lover in the night. She must have assumed that Calvin was sleeping, as it was long past midnight, but he had been sitting up in his study, reading over papers, unable to rest. When he heard the rattling of the wheels of a rapidly departing carriage, he had been struck by a sudden, inexplicable terror. The sound could have been made by anyone rushing by, but Calvin sensed that something was deeply wrong, and he went quickly to check on his daughters. Once he saw that both they and his wife were absent from their beds, his fears grew more concrete, and he raced to have a carriage of his own prepared to pursue them.

The process took too long. The horses were resting in their stables, not at all ready to be hooked up to the carriage, and Calvin paced frantically as he waited, demanding that the groomsman hitch the fastest horse to the fastest cart so that they could catch the absconders as quickly as possible. As soon as the horse was ready, he raced off into the night, forced to guess the direction that his wife had disappeared.

Fortunately—or perhaps unfortunately, considering the eventual outcome—his wife's carriage was slow and heavy, designed more for comfort for a rich woman and her two young children than for speed, and Calvin eventually spotted them moving ahead of his on the road. He could not know for certain that that lone carriage was the one he was pursuing, but it was the first carriage he had seen since leaving the heart of the city, and as soon as those in the carriage caught sight of him, they whipped their horses to greater speed.

The pursuit was on, but Calvin's wife and her lover would not give up easily. They forced their horses on, driving them past any reasonable speed, the carriage jerking from side to side on the road and tilted as they turned the corners. Despite their efforts, he was still gaining on them, and he shouted ahead, crying out for them to stop.

The driver whipped the horses again, and the whole carriage shuddered as the foaming creatures fought to attain even greater speed. A sharp turn in the road lay ahead, and Calvin shouted out in warning, but his words were lost in the wind.

One of the horses stumbled and veered toward the second. The second horse veered too, to escape its falling partner, and the sudden movement unbalanced the carriage behind them. The horses neighed in fright, and then there was a terrifying snap, as the harnesses that connected them to the carriage broke away. The horses continued to run, shaking with fear, while the carriage slid off the road. Calvin pushed his own horse forward, barely able to breathe as he watched the carriage collide with a stone wall that ran along the side of the road.

The crack was almost deafening. Calvin pulled his cart to a stop just beside it and ran over to the wreckage, terrified of what he might find. Maeve and Ethel were screaming. Ethel had a large bruise on her forehead, but Maeve seemed unharmed.

The same could not be said for his wife or her lover. Part of the carriage had crumpled, crushing the man, and his wife had been thrown violently by the force of the crash, and landed hard outside of the carriage. She was not moving, but Calvin could not be concerned by her wellbeing at that moment. He had to make certain his daughters were all right.

He scooped the two girls out of the wreckage as the carriage began to creak and sway again. Calvin threw his daughters free just in time. A moment later, the whole carriage overturned, trapping Calvin beneath its weight.

The girls were still screaming, and every one of Calvin's instincts told him to run to them and protect them, but he could not move from underneath the carriage. His whole body felt numb.

Hours passed before another person came along the road and found the wreckage. Luckily, they were a charitable soul, and they immediately stopped to help. The effort of a few men released Calvin from beneath the carriage, and a doctor was called. Calvin's rescuers would not allow him to move once he was out from the wreckage, in case his back was broken, but the doctor's eventual assessment was that Calvin had been very lucky, and that his spine had escaped any permanent damage.

The same could not be said for his leg. Although he could still walk, he would require a stick for the rest of his life, and the lingering pain never quite faded. He knew that he had become bitter in the months since the accident, made hard and cold by the pain and the betrayal, but his awareness of it was not enough to allow him to change. Perhaps, he thought, he had always been bitter and cold. Perhaps that was why his wife had left him. Perhaps his daughters would live better if he remained at a distance.

He had had difficulty keeping a nanny for his daughters, as he had explained to Mrs Green. Part of that was due to his daughters' unruliness since the accident, but part of that, he knew, was down to himself. When Mrs Green had written to him seeking a position for her young ward, he had written back without thinking, offering the job. The girls did need a nanny, after all, and perhaps a girl with Mrs Green's recommendation would last longer than the others had done.

The girl, when she arrived, was not what he had expected. She was meek and respectful, but she was bold too, daring to approach him with questions about the girls. She was beautiful, but she had an air of sadness about her that Calvin understood very well. Still, what could a young girl of her age have to be sad about? Whatever her problems were, they would heal with time and age. His could not be mended.

Calvin had barely seen the girl since the day after her arrival. She had been with them over a month now, which Calvin considered a good sign. He might finally have discovered someone who could handle his girls, which would be one less thing to concern himself about. But he began to wonder about this young woman who now had his daughters under her care. Could he really trust her, when so many others had failed him?

So, one evening, Calvin called the girl to his study. He noticed the change in her as soon as she walked through the door. Just as he had expected, she had already shed some of the sadness that had weighed her down when he first encountered her. He was surprised to realise that, instead of feeling bitter, he felt glad for her. Perhaps this house was capable of bringing someone joy, at least.

"Dora," he said. "Is that right?"

"Yes, sir," she said. She looked directly back at him, without demurring, and Calvin realised that there was something almost like anger in that look. He immediately felt that she did not like him.

"I wanted to hear how my daughters are progressing," Calvin said. "Are they well?"

"Why don't you go see them and find out for yourself, sir? I am sure that will answer your questions far better than I can."

The girl spoke softly, her tone polite, but the words brimmed with defiance. Calvin stared at her.

"You cannot tell me how my daughters are doing?"

"They are alive and fed," Dora said, "and they are well-cared-for with me. As for their spiritual wellbeing, Mr Adams, the picture is not so bright."

"What do you mean?"

"They are lonely, Mr Adams," she said. "They miss their parents. Ethel has given up her hopes of seeing you, but Maeve still holds on. They need their father."

Calvin frowned. "I am very busy," he said. "I pay you to ensure their needs are met."

"I can only do so much," Dora said. "I am not, and never can be, their father. I will do all I am able for these girls. I care for them very much. But it is not a replacement for a parent's love."

"And so you have come to berate me?" He was stunned by this young girl's nerve.

"I have answered your summons," Dora said, "and am now answering your inquiries too, by informing you that the girls' wellbeing would be improved if you came to check on it personally."

"And you think you have a right to tell me what to do?" Calvin asked.

"No, sir," Dora said. "But the girls are suffering. They need love. They need to see people and places outside of this household. It would be wrong of me not to say so, sir."

Calvin considered her. It stung, to be berated by such a young girl, and his first instinct was to deny all of her presumptuous claims. He remained distant from the girls *because* he loved them. They did not need poisoning with the bitterness of his presence, affected by whatever about him had ultimately driven his wife to run. He kept them inside because many people could not be trusted, and accidents were frequent in the world beyond these walls. He was protecting them.

Yet the girl's words stirred the guilt within him. Had he not known, all along, that the girls needed a father? Was that not part of why he was so bitter now, believing he had failed them?

"The girls do not need me," Calvin said.

"I respectfully disagree, sir," Dora said. "I believe they need you very much."

Calvin did not know what else to say to her. "You may go," he said, and she curtsied and departed without another word.

Calvin stared at the fire after she left, wishing his path was clear to him. Was there anything that he could do that would not harm his daughters? Was he doing them more harm than good, now, keeping them at arm's length?

Perhaps, he thought, there was merit in the girl's words. Perhaps it would be wise to speak to the girls himself and hear their thoughts on their new nanny and their activities. One visit, he was certain, would be enough to remind all involved that the girls were much better off without him.

CHAPTER TWENTY-THREE

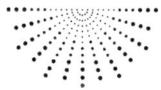

Dora lay awake in bed that night, unable to stop herself recounting her conversation with Mr Adams over and over again. What had possessed her to speak to him in such a way? She had been filled with defiant anger, fury at seeing how Mr Adams was hurting his daughters, and how little he seemed to truly value their wellbeing.

She would probably lose her position now. She could not go back to Colette and tell her that she had been dismissed. It would be an insult to all that Colette had done for her. She would have to find something else within York. But more than the security of the position, Dora found herself worrying about what would happen to Maeve and Ethel. She would miss the girls if she was forced to leave, and she thought that the girls might miss her too. Who would look after their well-being then?

But her angry summons never came, and the following evening, just as Dora was beginning to think that nothing would come of the encounter after all, Mr Finch arrived with a message. But it was not Dora that Mr Adams wished to see.

He wished to see his daughters.

Dora was so surprised that for a moment she did not move. Then her senses came back to her, and she ran over to the girls to try and ensure they looked presentable. Mr Finch coughed.

"The master would like to see them immediately, please," he said. And so, Dora was forced to shepherd the girls downstairs as-is and hope that Mr Adams would not find too much fault with their appearance.

Mr Adams was in his study again. Dora knocked on the door, and when Mr Adams said, "Enter," she pushed it open and guided the girls inside.

Mr Adams sat behind his desk, as he had the evening before. The fire roared in the grate behind him.

Ethel lingered by Dora's side, but Maeve immediately started running toward her father. "Papa!" she said. She threw her arms around his waist. "I have so much to tell you. We fought *monsters* today."

"Monsters?" Mr Adams asked, with a quirked eyebrow. "Goodness me."

"Maeve enjoys her games of make-believe, sir," Dora said.

"And why not?" Mr Adams replied, with more warmth and wonder in his voice than Dora had ever heard from him before. "A healthy imagination is good for a child."

"Ethel," Dora said, giving the older girl a little push. "Go and greet your father."

Ethel remained where she was. She crossed her arms and glared at her father with disapproval. "Why haven't you been to see us?" she asked him.

Mr Adams hesitated. "I have had a lot of work," he said eventually. "Adults have many things to keep them busy."

"You used to see us every day," Ethel said. "You used to talk to us and play with us. You were going to teach me how to read."

"I'm not a very good teacher," Mr Adams said. "I will get you a tutor—"

"You promised," Ethel said.

"Papa," Maeve said, pulling on his sleeve. "Papa, why can't we go to Mr Nichols's anymore? Dora brought us back some lemon drops, and they were really good."

"It isn't safe," Mr Adams said.

"It was safe before," Maeve insisted. "Papa, please. I want to go! And Ethel does too. *And* Dora."

"Well," Mr Adams said slowly. "If *Dora* wishes it, then who am I to deny her?"

Maeve frowned, trying to figure out whether that had been a yes or a no.

"On Sunday, you may go," he said eventually. "It—it has been too long since you girls were in church, so I think—you will go to church with Dora, and you may visit Mr Nichols's on your way home. Yes?"

"Yes!" Maeve said. She threw her arms around her father again. "Thank you, papa!"

Dora stared at him in amazement. What had inspired such a great change of heart? Had he truly listened to what she had told him? Listened to *her*, a nanny, an orphan? She was stunned.

"Now," Mr Adams said to his daughters, "I believe it is almost bedtime. Be good for Dora, won't you?"

"Yes, papa!" Maeve said. Ethel continued to stand by Dora's side and did not reply.

Dora lay awake again that night, but for an entirely different reason. She had seen a new aspect to Mr Adams that evening, one that she had truly never expected to see. Could it really have been because of her?

The following afternoon, she received word from Mr Finch again. Mr Adams wished to begin Ethel's reading lessons, if she were amenable. He asked that she come down to his study before supper so they could begin.

Ethel said little about the news, but Dora could see the hope that flickered to life within her as she prepared to go down again and see her father. It was the hope of a girl who had become cynical far too young in life, who had seen far more than such a young girl should ever see, and who was now faced with possibility again.

Their first outing that Sunday was also a great success. Maeve and Ethel both stayed close to Dora's side, but they gaped at all the sights as they walked, and Maeve's face wore a permanent grin. Mr Nichols greeted them warmly and snuck a few extra sweets into their paper bags, and Ethel looked so excited at all the jars of sweets that she almost cried.

The only problem arose as they walked back to their home, and a carriage rattled past them on the road, recklessly fast. Ethel turned as white as a sheet as she jumped back, and Maeve shrieked. It was an extreme reaction to a passing carriage, no matter how fast it was moving, and Dora quickly guided the two girls away, wondering what could have inspired it. Was this the accident that had scared them all so, taken away their mother and left Mr Adams unwilling to allow the girls to leave the home?

Although Dora hoped that Mr Adams's attention to the girls would last, she did not fully trust that it would. He had neglected the girls for so long that it seemed unlikely he would have a complete change of heart now.

Yet Ethel's reading lessons continued, and Maeve was invited to spend time with her father too. But the most surprising thing of all came on Dora's next day off. She wandered into the playroom in the late afternoon, expecting to find the girls running wild while a maid sat sulkily in the corner, and was shocked to find Mr Adams himself sitting in the warm armchair, a book in his hands and both daughters on his lap.

None of them looked up when Dora opened the door, all of them too absorbed in the story to notice her presence. Dora lingered for a moment, listening. Mr Adams's voice was rich and soothing, and Dora felt a rush of affection for him, and for the girls, as she listened to him speak. It made her want to lean against the doorframe, close her eyes, and get lost in the story too. But this was a private moment, and she did not wish to interrupt it.

Very quietly, she crept away.

CHAPTER TWENTY-FOUR

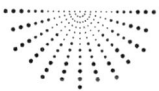

Slowly, day by day, Calvin Adams began to feel like a different man again. His leg still hurt him constantly, and he still mourned the past and all that he had lost, but every day spent with his daughters reminded him of all the blessings he still possessed, and of the possibility that he could do good as well as ill.

He had been certain that one meeting with his daughters would be enough to reassure everyone that they would be happier without his interference. He had not expected Maeve's excitement and effusion—and when had she grown so big?—eager to talk to him and tell him about her games, desperate for permission to leave the house again. But it had been Ethel's demeanour that had truly affected him. He remembered her as a quiet but cheerful girl, and fiercely intelligent for her age. The girl he saw in his study that day was just as intelligent, but those discerning eyes were now turned on him, and he saw sadness and disappointment there. She rebuked him for neglecting his promise to teach her, and Calvin reasoned that it was his fatherly duty to provide her with an education. A few sessions in his study in the evening would do no one any harm.

But again, he had underestimated his daughters. One lesson was enough to remind him of how intelligent and curious his older daughter was, and her quiet questions and quick progress made his heart swell with pride. As their sessions continued, Ethel began to warm up to him as well, and although she was not the carefree child he had known before the accident, she began to seem hopeful again.

Was it the accident that had caused such a severe change in his daughter, or was it Calvin's reaction to it, the isolation that followed? Calvin had been so lost in his belief that his girls would flourish without him that he had not paused to think that perhaps they would disagree.

He could thank Miss Dora Wentworth for that change of heart. She was surprisingly bold and insightful for one so young. But Calvin could not allow himself to think too fondly of the girl. Perhaps his daughters might need him after all, as he needed them, but a bright young thing like Dora Wentworth should not have to suffer his destructive influence any more than necessary.

This is what Calvin Adams told himself, and he almost believed it. But one evening, when Dora came to collect

Ethel from her lesson, he noticed her peering at the example letters that Ethel had been copying from Calvin's hand.

"She is coming along very well," Calvin said, and she nodded vaguely.

"I—I would not know," she said. "I do not read well myself. Mrs Green has been sending me letters, but—it is difficult to read them, and impossible for me to reply."

"You do not know how to read?" Calvin asked. He was astounded. She was such an intelligent girl.

"Not beyond the basics," Dora said. "When I lived at a church orphanage, they taught us some letters. But once my aunt and uncle adopted me, I did not receive any schooling again." She looked at Ethel's work again, almost wistfully.

"Would you like to learn?" Calvin asked, before he could stop himself.

"Sir?"

"Come," Calvin said. "I will teach you."

Dora blushed scarlet. "Oh, I couldn't impose—"

"Nonsense," Calvin said. Now that he was set on the idea, he could not imagine things going any other way. "It will benefit us all for you to learn. Ethel, would you mind if Dora joined us for lessons sometimes?"

"No," Ethel said. She smiled. "Not at all."

"Then it is settled," Calvin said.

Dora's mind raced as she led Ethel back upstairs. She did not understand why Mr Adams would be concerned with something as irrelevant to him as her education. Rich men were eccentric, she supposed. But for him to go from a man who would barely speak to her, a man who never saw his children, to a man who offered to teach her how to read... the transformation seemed impossible. Had he never been the man she had first perceived him to be? And if that were the case, why had he acted so coldly before?

Dora felt the danger of getting any closer to such an enigmatic man. But she could not refuse such an invitation, if it was sincere. She would once again gain something she had been missing her entire life. First, she had gained Ethel and Maeve. Now she would learn to read.

But Ethel's young mind was far quicker at grasping her lessons than Dora's. Her brain buzzed when she stared at the shapes on the page, reading each letter one by one while Ethel devoured entire words. Dora was certain that she would have to leave Ethel's lessons, for all of their sakes, and was shocked again when Mr Adams asked if she would be willing to work alone together instead, after the girls had gone to sleep.

Dora grew up around inappropriate comments and leering men, so she was not naive, and was particularly sensitive to when a man had ill intent, but she sensed none of that from Mr Adams when he gave her the invitation. He seemed sincere and scholarly, offering a polite and tentative suggestion that was all for her own benefit. Dora did not know what to think of it. She did not know how to behave around this mysterious man when they were alone.

But Dora wanted to learn, and so she agreed.

Soon, Dora and Mr Adams were spending almost every evening together, leaning over books. He was a patient teacher, and she found herself learning quickly, eager to read more words and to discuss them with him. As time passed, she grew to value the handsomeness of his expression and the steady tone of his voice. She found she missed him if a day passed when she did not see him.

The more time Dora spent with him, the more she realised that he was a kind and patient and generous man. He never spoke to her about the past, about the accident that had taken his wife from them and left him with so much pain, but Dora sensed that it had changed him, and that now, with time, his real self was beginning to emerge again.

Dora had to remind herself not to get caught up in her thoughts, however. Mr Adams was her employer, not her companion. He did not think of her as anything more than his children's uneducated nanny, she was certain, as a silly girl who spoke out of turn and did not even know how to read. Growing attached to him would only lead to heartbreak, and she knew that her heart would be broken enough the day that Mr Adams decided his girls no longer needed her. Maeve and Ethel felt like her family now, and her greatest source of sadness now was that their time together would not last forever.

For now, however, she tried to live in the moment, and savour every second of happiness that she could.

CHAPTER TWENTY-FIVE

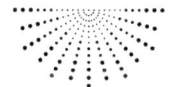

One evening, a few weeks later, Dora sat in Ethel and Maeve's bedchamber, stroking the younger girl's hair to help soothe her to sleep.

"Dora?" Maeve said sleepily.

"Hush, now," Dora said. "It's bedtime. We can talk tomorrow."

"Don't leave, Dora," Maeve mumbled.

"I'll be here until you fall asleep," Dora promised, but Maeve shook her head.

"Don't leave us at all. Everyone always leaves… I want you to stay."

"Then I'll stay," Dora said, running her fingers through Maeve's hair. "I promise I will."

She leaned forward and kissed Maeve's forehead. Just as Maeve had drifted off to sleep, and Dora was thinking of retiring herself, she heard a loud thud from the stairs. With a quick glance at the girls to make sure that neither of them had awoken, Dora hurried from the room in search of the source of the noise.

What she found made her gasp in horror. Mr Adams lay sprawled at the bottom of the staircase, moaning in pain.

"Mr Adams!" Dora cried. She flew down the stairs to his side. He was conscious, at least, but his eyes rolled beneath his eyelids, and he did not speak in response. Instead, he just groaned loudly again.

More footsteps hurried down the hallway, and Mr Finch appeared. "I don't know what happened," Dora said frantically. "I heard a crash and he was lying here. I think he fell. Mr Finch, we must call the doctor!"

"We must move him first," Mr Finch said. "Can you help me, Miss Wentworth? My old back will not support his weight if I try to lift him alone."

Dora slid her arm under one of Mr Adam's shoulders while Mr Finch slid his under the other. Dora had never touched Mr Adams before, not even a brush of the hands, but she was far too panicked to think about the inappropriateness of what she was doing now. Together, she and Mr Finch dragged Mr Adams into his bedchamber and laid him atop his bed.

"I will fetch the doctor," Mr Finch said. "I will return as quickly as I am able."

Dora barely looked away from Mr Adams as Mr Finch took his leave. His footsteps faded down the corridor, leaving the only sounds as the ticking of the clock and Mr Adams's laboured breathing. Mr Adams groaned again, as though in great pain, and Dora instinctively smoothed her hand over his hair, like she might for Maeve or Ethel when they were unwell.

"Hush now," she said. "Don't you worry, Mr Adams. Mr Finch has gone for the doctor. You will be all right." She could not tell whether Mr Adams could hear or understand her, but she felt a little calmer as she spoke. She could only hope that her words were reaching him somehow.

Where was Mr Finch with the doctor? How long had it now been? It felt like it had been an eternity, but in reality it had probably only been five or ten minutes. How long would it take to fetch him? Would he come straight away?

Sweat pooled on Mr Adams's brow, and Dora hurried to fetch a bowl of water and a cloth to dab it with. What had happened to him? All Dora knew was that Mr Adams could not die. Maeve and Ethel could not become orphans. Dora would not allow it.

The doctor finally arrived, and Dora was hurried out of the room so that he could perform his examination. Dora sat down on the floor of the hallway outside Mr Adams's room and waited. She hoped that the two girls were still asleep. Perhaps, by the time they awoke in the morning, the fear would be over and their father would be with them again.

It was not to be. The doctor spent an age with Mr Adams, and although he did not speak with Dora as he departed, Dora knew from his grave expression that the news was not good.

"Mr Finch?" she asked, when the butler returned from seeing the doctor out. The man looked as though he had aged ten years in the past half an hour. "What is wrong with him? Will he be all right?"

"He is weak," Mr Finch said. "All we can do is wait and see how he is when he wakes."

It was not the answer that Dora had hoped for, but it was better than her worst fears. All she could do now was stay beside him and try to encourage him to wake.

Dora stayed beside Mr Adams all night, placing cool water on his brow and murmuring words of hope and support.

When the girls awoke the following morning, Dora had no choice but to tell them the news about their father's condition. Maeve cried and asked Dora if their father was going to leave them, while Ethel simply went very quiet and looked down at the ground without speaking. In the face of Maeve's tears, Dora found herself promising that their father would recover, but in truth, she knew that it was far from certain. She tried to focus on distracting the girls, playing games with Maeve and asking Ethel to teach her what she knew about reading and writing, but Dora's thoughts lingered downstairs in the sickroom of her employer.

As soon as the girls were asleep at the end of the day, Dora hurried back to Mr Adams's side. There had been no change in his condition. Dora brushed the hair back from his forehead and looked at his face, currently smooth and untroubled in sleep. Surely that was a good sign, was it not? He did not seem to be suffering.

When, she wondered, had her feelings about her employer changed? She had thought him so cold and unloving at first, but now her heart wept at the thought of losing him. And Dora could not deceive herself. She wept for the girls, for all that they had lost and all that they might lose still, but that was not the full extent of her heartbreak. Mr Adams was a kind man, beneath all of his pain. Dora had not seen the truth before, but now she knew that she loved him.

He would never love her, of course. She was a poor, uneducated girl without family. He might be kind to her and accept her into his household to care for his children, but she knew she could not gain a place in his heart. But Dora was accustomed to heartbreak and loneliness. Her greatest hope now was that Mr Adams would live.

Tears streaming down her face, Dora leaned forward and pressed a chaste kiss to Mr Adams's lips. "Fight this," she whispered to him. "You have to live. Please."

CHAPTER TWENTY-SIX

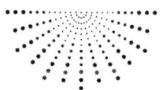

Calvin slipped in and out of consciousness for many days. Each time his senses returned to him, he felt as though he were experiencing the world through a great fog, and his eyelids were too heavy for him to open them. Nothing felt entirely real.

Yet, through the fog, Calvin sensed a figure watching over him. He felt a gentle hand on his brow, and heard the voice of an angel encouraging him, singing to him, even reading in a hesitant but determined tone. The angel brushed the hair from his forehead, and sometimes even kissed him gently on the lips, whispering that she loved him and urging him to recover.

Calvin could not have said how long he remained in the fog. Sometimes it faded a little when the angel was there, only to come rushing back later, engulfing him again. But after some unknowable length of time, Calvin awoke to find that the fog had gone. He opened his heavy eyelids and blinked in the sunlight that streamed in through his window. He was currently alone.

If he called out, he knew someone would come running. But as Calvin took in the room, he noticed a chair placed closed to his bedside, and a book on the table that he was certain had not been there before. He remembered the angel who had watched over him through the fog. Had that been a mere dream? Or had someone truly come to care for him, kissed him, even told him they loved him?

It must have been his fevered mind, reaching for dreams that could never be his reality. No one would treat him that way. Yet he looked at that chair and that book, and he wondered.

Then he heard gentle footsteps and voices from the hallway outside his room. Was that his angel returning? Calvin closed his eyes and calmed his breathing as the door creaked open. He did not wish to deceive, but in his heart he knew that he must learn the truth.

Three sets of footsteps entered the room. "There, you see?" Dora said. "He looks peaceful. He is just resting."

For a moment, Calvin thought that his deception had been detected. But then Maeve asked: "Then why won't he wake up?"

"He will," Dora said. "When he is ready. Come on. Let's keep him company. See if we can encourage him to wake."

He heard the sound of Dora settling in the chair beside the bed, while his two daughters climbed onto the bed beside him and curled up, one on either side of him. They rested their heads on his chest, burrowing their faces into the soft blanket, and Dora picked up the book from the bedside table and began to read.

It was a book of fairy tales; not the sort of thing that Calvin would choose to read himself, but a good tale for the children. Although Dora still stumbled over the occasional word, her voice rang clear and pure like a bell as she read, and Calvin found himself captivated by the rhythm of her words. His daughters' breathing slowed as the story lulled them to sleep, but Calvin remained aware. Was this what he had heard in his dreams? Dora's love and concern for his daughters, misinterpreted by his foggy mind as love and concern for him?

When Dora finished the story, she set the book gently back on the table and then leaned forward and gently brushed the hair away from Calvin's head. She pressed a gentle kiss to the skin there, and then kissed his lips. "I know you can recover," she whispered to him. "Please try, sir. For your daughters, and—and for me. I love you, sir. All of you. Please get better. For them, and for me."

Dora leaned back and fell silent again, but Calvin could not rest. His dream had been true. Dora loved him. This beautiful, kind-hearted young woman felt love for a mean, bitter old man like him. It seemed impossible. He could not believe it. But why would she lie in a moment like this, when she believed she was alone?

She was so strong and so loving. But Calvin knew, deep in his heart, that he did not deserve her love.

When Dora came to his room the next day, Calvin opened his eyes. Dora let out a squeak of surprise, her face turning scarlet. "Mr Adams!" she said. "You're awake. I—I will just fetch Mr Finch, if you'll give me a moment—"

"No," Calvin said. His voice croaked from disuse. "Stay. Please. I must speak with you."

"With me, sir?" Dora asked. She took a tentative step forward. "What do you want with me?"

"You cared for me," Calvin said. His tone made clear that it was not a question. "You kept me alive."

"I—" Fear darted across Dora's face. "Sir, I—"

"I am not angry, Dora," he said. "I am grateful."

"Oh," Dora said. Her face was still red, and tears glinted in her eyes. "Then—then you are welcome, sir."

"Will you call me Calvin?" he asked. "Please."

"I—I'm not certain it would be proper, sir."

"You saved my life," he said. "I think that should place us on first-name terms with one another, don't you?"

"I—what do you remember?" she asked him, taking another tentative step forward.

"I remember you caring for me," Calvin said. "I remember you bringing in the girls and reading to us. I remember you brushing the hair from my forehead and kissing my lips and telling me that you loved me. Is it true, Dora? Did you truly mean that?"

Dora considered him for a moment with wide eyes. Then, slowly, she nodded. "Yes," she said. "I meant every word."

Calvin's heart sang at her confession, but the darkness and self hatred within him still tugged at his thoughts, insisting it could not be. A bright young woman like Dora could not love a ruined man like him.

"Please," he said. "Will you sit with me?"

Dora nodded and walked slowly to the chair where she had held vigil all these nights.

"How long was I unwell?" Calvin asked her.

"Almost two weeks," Dora said. "I was afraid that you might never wake."

"But now I am here again," Calvin said. "Thanks to your assistance."

Dora shook her head. "I did nothing," she said. But Calvin knew that was not true.

"Dora," he said. "Since you arrived in this house, you have shown me things that I had for too long forgotten. You made me see my own selfishness and neglect, how I was allowing fear to control me and to inflict greater suffering on my daughters. I feared losing them so deeply that I almost lost them through my own actions. I—do not know what you know of our story."

"Very little, sir," Dora said.

Calvin nodded. She needed to know the truth. Surely that would show her the error of her feelings, make her see him as he truly deserved to be seen. "For many months," he said, "I kept a distance from my daughters. You see, I feared—I feared that they were not my children at all. My wife had a secret lover, you see, and once I learned of it, it was impossible for me to know whether my daughters were a product of my love, as I had believed, or of betrayal. Their mother attempted to flee with her lover and the girls, and when I pursued them... there was an accident. A carriage accident. I rescued my daughters, but my wife was killed, and I was grievously injured in the crash. It still causes me pain. So I became bitter and fearful. I feared the girls' dying, but I also feared losing them due to the truth about their birth. It was you, Dora, who helped me to see the error in that. I cannot thank you enough for all you have done for us."

Dora reached forward and took his hand in hers. "You do not need to thank me," she said. "I have done little. But I know a little of what it is to feel as your daughters must have felt, and perhaps a little of your own feelings too. I do not know how much Mrs Green told you of my background, or how much of it she knew herself, but I was an unwanted child. A fisherman found me abandoned in the river, soon after I was born, and he and his wife took me in. I do not know the identities of my mother and father, or what caused them to throw me aside as they did. For a couple of years, I had a family. But then the fisherman and his wife—they could not care for me either, and they took me to an orphanage. For a long time, I believed that it must have been my fault. If I had been a better child, they would not have abandoned me. But I do not believe that anymore. Life is difficult, and we all act as we believe is best, even if it ends up hurting those we would never normally wish to hurt. I believe they must have had their reasons, too. They must have believed it would help me, not hurt me."

"But it did hurt you," Calvin said.

Dora nodded. "My carers meant well," she said, "but there were too many children to care for, and not enough time or money available to give us more than we needed to survive. When a family came to find a child to adopt, the orphanage gave me away without a thought, and although I thought I might finally have a family again, I was wrong. They did not love me. They simply wanted to use me.

"But now—now I have found a family, here. I love Ethel and Maeve very much. And you, Calvin, you are—" She paused, tears glinting in her eyes. "In the end, it does not matter that I do not know who my natural father is. I have a Father in Heaven, and he has sustained me. He has protected me, and in his mercy, he brought me here. I had all that I needed, right from the beginning."

Calvin felt tears forming in his own eyes too. Faced with Dora's bravery and conviction, his guilt stung him more than ever, how he had hurt those most dear to him by closing off his heart and abandoning faith. Dora shone like a beacon of goodness before him.

She leaned forward now and took his hand. "Ethel and Maeve are wonderful children," she said, "devoted to God and to you. You are truly blessed to have them, as I am blessed to have found them. You see, I—I have injuries of my own. In the incident that led me to leave my adoptive home and meet Mrs Green, my uncle pushed me from a window. The fall nearly killed me. I survived, but—I can never have children. I know that would make me unacceptable as a wife to many men. But if you will have me, Calvin, I will be a good mother to your girls. I swear that I will."

Calvin released her hand. His hope faded, and his doubt and self-loathing surged again. Dora could not truly love him. She loved the girls, yes, and she wished to be with them, but she would realise her mistake regarding him soon enough. She loved his daughters, and she longed for a family, but she could find a far better man than Calvin.

Dora frowned at him in confusion. "I must rest," Calvin said. "Please inform Mr Finch that I am awake."

"Oh," Dora said. She looked away, and another tear rolled down her cheek. "Of course, sir. I will fetch him at once."

CHAPTER TWENTY-SEVEN

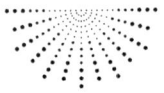

Dora cried greatly that night, and for many nights that followed. Even as her heart broke, she cursed herself for her selfishness. Calvin was awake and recovered. The girls would have their father again. It had been her own foolishness that had allowed her to build this fantasy while caring for him, the dream that perhaps he might grow to love her too. The dream that she might have found a family here.

She hid her pain from Maeve and Ethel, but when they went to visit their father, she did not accompany them. Calvin—Mr Adams—did not call for Dora again, and she would not impose on him, when he had made his feelings clear. He had responded to her confession with a dismissal, and she would need to accept it.

Still, Dora was greatly relieved when she received a note from Colette Green, speaking of her intention to visit.

Colette was concerned for Mr Adams and wished to apply her nursing knowledge to his case, and she also wished to see Dora and discover how she was finding her new life. Dora did not intend to share one word of disappointment or complaint with her friend, but she longed for her presence. Once she arrived, Dora thought she might feel less alone again.

Colette embraced her young friend as soon as she saw her, exclaiming that she looked far too thin. Dora made her excuses while Colette went to see Mr Adams, but Colette soon returned, declaring their need to take a stroll together.

"Now, come, Dora," Colette said, as they walked arm in arm together down the cobbled streets of the city. "I may be old, but I am no fool. Something is troubling you. Perhaps I can be of help."

"It is nothing," Dora said softly. "Just young foolishness. Do not concern yourself with it."

"Is it something related to our friend, Mr Adams?" Colette asked with a gentle smile. "He is changed since I last saw him. Withdrawn, but in a different manner. Perhaps you had something to do with it?"

"I care for his children," Dora said. "And that is all I will ever be to him." She sighed wistfully.

"Ah," Colette said. "It is as I suspected. A matter of the heart. Come now, Dora. Tell me. I was young once too, you know. What is the matter? Do you fear he does not return your affection? Because from his disappointment that you did not join me on my visit to his chambers, I rather think you are mistaken."

"There is no mistake, Colette," Dora said. "He—he is aware of my feelings, and he has rejected them."

"Rejected them?" Colette asked. "I find that difficult to believe."

"Please believe me," Dora said, "for it is the truth. We spoke when he awoke from his illness. At first, it—it seemed hopeful. He had sensed how I cared for him while he was recovering, and he asked me of my feelings. He told me more about the accident that led to his wife's death, and I—I told him some more of my life before I came here. It seemed hopeful. I was so afraid, but I plucked up the courage to tell him of my feelings, of my injury, and of how I could not give him more children, but how we could all be a family together. How I wished for that more than anything. But once I said it—he sent me away. He gave no real response, but his silence and his dismissal were response enough. He has not called for me since, and I have not been to visit him. He does not care for me."

"What is this foolishness?" Colette said. "Calvin does not open his heart or speak of the accident to anyone. He could not tell you of it without having deep and sincere feelings for you as well."

"I do not know what to tell you," Dora said. "It all happened exactly as I have described. He does not love me, Colette. My greatest fear now is that he will send me away for my boldness. and I will lose the girls as well as him."

"If he did that," Colette said, "he would be an even greater fool than he has already proven himself to be. I will get to the bottom of this, Dora."

"No," Dora said, clutching her arm. "Please don't. He has made his feelings clear."

But Colette had lived many years and seen many things, and she liked to think of herself as a good judge of both character and affection. Both Dora and Calvin had been despondent upon her arrival, mirrors of one another's sadness. She suspected that it was stubbornness and fear, not a lack of affection, that had stalled the match, and nothing would make her more pleased now than contributing to the future happiness of her two friends by forcing them both to see the truth.

But Dora, she saw, would not listen. Calvin had dismissed her, and the girl had taken it to heart. Colette would need to speak to Calvin herself to solve this issue.

As soon as they returned to the house and Dora left to care for the children, Colette marched to Calvin's study. She rapped sharply on the door, and barely waited for his response before marching inside.

Calvin sat working at his desk, his back to the roaring fire. He glanced up when Colette entered, but Colette did not give him the opportunity to speak.

"What is this I have been hearing," she said, "about you pushing Dora away?"

Calvin looked back at his papers. "I do not know what you are talking about," he said. Colette marched over to him. "Stop this foolishness," she said. "You have a good, kind-hearted, generous girl who loves you very much. Do not tell me you do not love her in return, because your face reveals your truth."

Calvin shook his head. "She does not love me," he said. "She loves the girls, and she thinks herself in love with me, but she will see her error soon enough."

"And you think you know the girl's own heart and mind better than she knows them herself?"

"I do," Calvin said. "She revealed it when she spoke to me. She wishes for a family, and she loves my daughters. She would not be happy when she realised she had married me to achieve that dream."

"She loves *you*," Colette said. "I know it to be true, and I believe you know it as well. You are simply afraid."

"And if I am?" Calvin asked. "What is the harm in that?"

"The harm?" Colette repeated. "The harm is the pain it causes not just to you and to Dora, but to the girls as well.

You must open your eyes, Calvin. You are allowing your fear to deceive you again. Can you not see our Lord's merciful hand in all of this? In my finding Dora, in her coming into your employ, in all that has happened since? He has provided you with a wonderful, loving wife, and a wonderful mother for your children, if only you will climb out of your own pit of pity and see it."

Calvin gaped at her.

"My words may be harsh," Colette continued, "but they are true, and you must hear them. The girl loves you, and you love her. Do not hurt yourself from fear and push her away."

Colette left without another word to rejoin her friend and play with the girls, but her words lingered in Calvin's heart. What a fool he had been. He only hoped it was not too late to make amends.

CHAPTER TWENTY-EIGHT

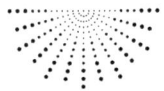

The weekend came, and Dora prepared the girls for their Sunday outing to church. But as Dora was fastening Maeve's coat, Mr Adams appeared.

"I was hoping I might join you," he said, a little nervously.

"Of course," Dora said, as calmly as she could manage, but her heart was beating wildly in her chest. Mr Adams had never joined them before. What could he mean by joining them now?

It must be for his daughters, she told herself. It could not possibly be for her. But then Mr Adams looked at her and gave her a small smile, and she felt herself smiling back, hope blooming in her heart once again.

They did not talk much as they walked to church, although Maeve chattered wildly. Calvin listened attentively to the morning's sermon, and when he knelt to pray, Dora shepherded the girls away to give him the peace and focus he clearly desired. A tear rolled down his cheek as he spoke to the Lord, and Dora distracted the girls, knowing he would not wish to be observed.

Afterward, they walked to the sweet shop and then back to the manor, and still Calvin did not speak. Dora left him to his thoughts. By the end of the outing, she had convinced herself that their meeting was a coincidence, that Calvin had merely intended to leave the house himself to pray and felt it rude to abandon them once he saw them in the hallway. But when they reached the manor's gates, Calvin paused.

"Maeve and Ethel," he said. "Why don't you run ahead inside, and tell Miss Beth what you learned today at church? I must speak with Dora."

The girls scampered away, but not before Ethel gave her nanny a far too knowing and delighted glance.

"Will you walk with me?" Calvin asked her. He sounded a little uncertain, almost shy, as he held out his arm for her to take.

Dora nodded and slid her arm through his. They walked slowly together down the cobbled street toward the park.

"Is everything all right, sir?" Dora asked him, in a soft voice.

"Dora," he said. "Please. I've asked you to call me Calvin."

"All right," Dora said, a little hesitantly. "Calvin."

"Dora, I've been a fool," Calvin said. "I have been so afraid of being hurt again that I have pushed everyone away, including yourself. I could not believe that such a good, kind-hearted young woman such as yourself could ever truly care for a man such as me."

"I do care for you," Dora said. "Very much."

"I realise my error now," Calvin said. "I have hurt so many people around me. You were the first to show me that, Dora. I hope that you can forgive me for all I have done."

"It is already forgiven," Dora said. "I do not wish to worry about the past. The future is all I wish to concern myself with."

"Then let us think of the future," Calvin said. "Ever since the Lord brought you into my life, Dora, everything has been different. I feel hope again. I love you, Dora Wentworth. And if you would have me, I hope you will do me the honour of agreeing to become my wife."

Dora stared at Calvin in amazement. "Be your wife?" she repeated. It was such an impossible idea. She had barely dared to dream that such words might ever come her way. For so long, she had felt herself broken, unlovable. She had longed for and dreamed of a family of her own, a family she knew she would almost certainly never have. And now, for Calvin to offer all that she had dreamed of, after initially seeming to reject her... she could not quite believe it. "Do you truly mean it?" she whispered.

"I have never been so sincere about anything in all my life," Calvin said. He slowly knelt and looked up at her with an earnest expression. "Please, marry me, Dora."

"Calvin!" Dora said. "You'll hurt yourself."

"I need you to see how sincere I am, Dora. And you deserve all the romance of a true proposal. I will not rise until I receive your response. Will you marry me?"

Dora knelt down on the ground before him. "Yes," she said. Tears of joy rolled down her cheeks. "Yes, Calvin. Of course, I will marry you."

Calvin reached forward and cupped her face with his palm.

"Is this really happening?" Dora whispered.

"Yes," Calvin said. "I assure you that it is."

He leaned forward and kissed her sweetly on the lips, and Dora smiled.

CHAPTER TWENTY-NINE

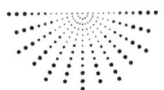

Calvin and Dora were wed a few weeks later, with Colette and both daughters in attendance. Colette bought Dora a beautiful new dress for the occasion, and once the ceremony was concluded, Ethel and Maeve both embraced Dora with such enthusiasm that she was almost knocked off her feet.

After the wedding, the new family travelled to the coast—by steam train, not carriage—and delighted in playing on the shorefront together. They tried many fairground games, collected shells along the rocky beach, and visited the monuments and ruins that overlooked the rough, wind-tossed sea. Dora's heart sang with joy every day, and Calvin's past kindness and exuberance shone through as he delighted in time spent with his daughters and his new wife.

When the family returned to their home in York, Dora would not even think of them acquiring a new nanny for the girls. She wanted to be even more involved in the lives and the upbringing of her new daughters than she had been before, and with their mother and father as their steady, caring and patient guardians, Ethel and Maeve never had to feel lonely or unloved again.

And a few months after the wedding, another miracle occurred. Despite being assured that she would never have children of her own, her growing signs of pregnancy became too clear to be ignored, and her new doctor confirmed what she had thought would never be. Dora was pregnant. Dora watched her growing belly over the next few months with awe and delighted in sitting with her hand on the bump, feeling the wriggles and kicks of her child.

Some of Calvin's old fears of loss returned as the time for the birth drew nearer, but Dora reminded him to have faith, and soon she was delivered of not one but two healthy baby boys. Dora watched the babes in wonder, marvelling at their tiny eyelashes and little grasping fingers.

They named the boys Martin and Edgar, and Maeve and Ethel were delighted by their new siblings. The family lived happily together for the rest of their days, and although they faced difficulties, as all families do, they faced them with a certainty in God's care and in one another's love. They guided one another through the hard times, and supported each other through the good, and Dora savoured every day, knowing that the Lord was watching over her, and that dreams really could come true.

THANK YOU FOR CHOOSING A PUREREAD BOOK!

We hope you enjoyed the story, and as a way to thank you for choosing PureRead we'd like to send you this free book, and other fun reader rewards…

Click here for your free copy of Whitechapel Waif
PureRead.com/victorian

Thanks again for reading.
See you soon!

LOVE VICTORIAN ROMANCE?

If you enjoyed this story why not continue straight away with other books in our PureRead Victorian Romance library?

Read them all...

Orphan Christmas Miracle

An Orphan's Escape

The Lowly Maiden's Loyalty

Ruby of the Slums

The Dancing Orphan's Second Chance

Cotton Girl Orphan & The Stolen Man

Victorian Slum Girl's Dream

The Lost Orphan of Cheapside

Dora's Workhouse Child

Saltwick River Orphan

Workhouse Girl and The Veiled Lady

OUR GIFT TO YOU

AS A WAY TO SAY THANK YOU WE WOULD LOVE TO SEND YOU THIS BEAUTIFUL STORY FREE OF CHARGE.

Our Reader List is 100% FREE

Click here for your free copy of Whitechapel Waif

PureRead.com/victorian

At PureRead we publish books you can trust. Great tales without smut or swearing, but with all of the mystery and romance you expect from a great story.

Be the first to know when we release new books, take part in our fun competitions, and get surprise free books in your inbox by signing up to our Reader list.

As a thank you you'll receive an exclusive copy of Whitechapel Waif - a beautiful book available only to our subscribers...

Click here for your free copy of Whitechapel Waif

PureRead.com/victorian

Printed in Great Britain
by Amazon